DEATH IN T

CW00422211

Copyright Page

Published in 2019 by CreateSpace

Copyright © 2019 Joe Harding

First Edition

ISBN- 9781686783210

Foreword

Devotees of the Ffestiniog and Welsh Highland Railway, a narrow-gauge railway that traverses the wild open spaces and deep valleys of North Wales, will be best equipped to judge if this book is a fair and accurate reflection of the company and its modus operandi. To them, I offer a qualified apology;

Death in the Last Carriage is essentially a story. One of the unwritten rules of storytelling is never to let the facts get in the way of a good tale. To this end I have played fast and loose with company procedures, occasionally moved the scenery around to provide a smooth flow of events and probably driven a coach and horses through cherished safety procedures.

But that aside, I leave you, the reader, to decide whether Death in the Last Carriage fulfils its intended purpose which is first and foremost to entertain, but also to inform and allow the reader to appreciate the Railway and the stunning surroundings it operates in just that little more. If, like myself, you hold an annual pass to the railway, you will be able to settle yourself into one of the carriages on a train leaving the Porthmadog Harbour Station, order a coffee and snack from the buffet and watch the Maentwrog Valley rattle past the window. And you will be able to share the adventure of DI Byron Unsworth as the events, like the train, gather pace.

Perhaps, too, as a result of reading this novel, you might be encouraged to walk around the region, to explore the mountains and the valleys and understand how the need for natural resources shaped this part of the world. But hopefully you will avoid some of the mishaps that overtake our characters in the book.

Joe Harding 2019

By the same author

The Swordsman of Calais 1 – Commission
The Swordsman of Calais 2 – Dissension
Timescope
Past; Tense (short stories)
Ouroboros (short stories)
All available on Kindle from Amazon

Death in the Last Carriage

Joe Harding

ACKNOWLEDGMENTS

Appreciation must be shown to those who willingly give their time to read my literary efforts:

Rosalind Winter – herself a capable writer and whose words of encouragement are always welcome

Beka White who loves a good detective story

Esther who always produces stunning book covers

And Sue Hare who always wants to read more.

Thank you.

When I created DI Byron Unsworth as an incidental player in the Ouroboros short story collection, I immediately felt a liking for him and the need to bring him more to life; to flesh out his character and background.

This tale is the result. I hope you found it enjoyable. If you wish to read a little more of our hero, then you can see him in action in the title story 'Ouroboros.'

I think DI Unsworth has more adventures awaiting him….

Place name pronunciation

The Welsh language can be a bit daunting if you are not familiar with the rules. To make it simple, the place names used in this book are rendered phonetically below: (source – Festipedia)

Penrhyndeudraeth	Pen-hrin-DYE-Dry-TH
Minffordd	MEAN-forth
Tanygrisiau	Tan-uh-GRISH-ya
Tan y Bwlch	Tan-uh-bullch
Blaenau Ffestiniog	BLIGH-na Fes-TIN-iog
Maentwrog	Mine-TOOR-og
Porthmadog	Porth-MAD-og
Beddgelert	Beth-GEL-ert
Garnedd (tunnel)	GARR-neth
Moelwyn (tunnel)	MOIL-win
Rhiw Goch	Hroo-GOCH
Caernarfon	Kire-NAR-von
Trawsfynnedd	TRAWS-fin-eth
Cnicht	CUH-nicked
Ysbyty Alltwen	Uss-butty Ol-twen
Pwllheli	Pu-THEL-EE
Tonfanau	Ton-van-eye
Stwlan	Stew-lan
Croesor	KROY-sore

CHAPTER 1

'LADIES AND GENTLEMEN, once again, our apologies for the delay. We should be getting underway in the next minute or two, just as soon as we have propped the fence up.'

A ragged, if slightly inebriated, cheer went up from the first class observation compartment. Not that anyone was really bothered by an unscheduled thirty-five minute halt. They were on holiday and Byron Unsworth had instructed Marta to keep them supplied with refreshments. The delay, though irritating, had boosted the buffet car takings considerably.

With a lurch David Lloyd George shot forward, the creak of couplings rattling back along the train as the carriages moved forward, gathering pace on the long gentle downhill towards Tan y Bwlch and onward to Porthmadog where the grumpy train crew would haul her off to clean out her firebox and ready her for tomorrow. They were late, so the maintenance crew would be late for their two or three pints at Spooners. Having no one else to blame they would rib him about the tardy timekeeping.

'What was it this time, Byron, lad? Left the carriages behind? Long queue in Blaenau chippy?'

The trouble was, Byron reflected, the actual reason for the extensive delay was so commonplace no one would believe it for a moment. Sheep were forever straying onto the permanent way; finding holes in wire fences or jumping over sagging sections in their insane urge to be crushed by oncoming locomotives. It was not as though the grass was any greener on the other side of the fence – quite the opposite, the track was sparsely grassed. It was just in their woolly DNA to disrupt any attempt at running an organised service on the Ffestiniog Railway.

They were clear of Moelwyn Tunnel now, the high sides of the cutting opening out on his left into the gentler slopes of upper

Dduallt where the original railway track bed marched out of the old tunnel and strode self-importantly across the sheep-dotted fields. On the way up the skies had been clear and he had taken a moment to gaze at the wide valley with its tree lined lower slopes, brooded over in the far distance by the brutal bulk of Trawsfyndd Nuclear Power Station. But since their unscheduled halt in Moelwyn Tunnel the weather had abruptly changed its mind and decided to test the local roofs to see if the slate was as good as the residents claimed it to be. A vicious wind slammed huge drops against the windows and the view reduced to a grey blanket.

Leaving the rarefied atmosphere of First Class Observation, he manoeuvred his bulk through the narrow, draughty sections between the next sets of carriages, repeating his profound apologies to the scattering of passengers and checking if anyone needed further refreshments. In the fourth carriage back a door window and two table windows were wide open and the seats already soaking wet. With a grunt of annoyance, Byron snapped them shut wondering as he did so whether those responsible routinely left their windows open at home when they left.

Marta, trawling the carriages from the other direction with a notebook picking up food and drink orders noticed the pools of water on the varnished tables.

'Leave that to me,' she smiled. 'I'll do it when I come back.'

'Thanks, Marta.' Byron had two types of volunteers he regularly dealt with – those who he would gladly welcome back, and those he would wish never to see again. Marta was firmly in the first category. 'Get yourself a drink as well – you've earned it!'

She flashed him her shy smile, trying to hide her crooked front teeth and slipped back towards the buffet car. The train was rounding the last curve of the Loop and heading past Dduallt station. Not surprisingly no one was waiting to be collected or dropped off. Byron checked his watch. No need to wait long at Tan y Bwlch – theirs was the last service on this Saturday evening so with luck they might recover a few minutes.

In the fifth carriage a boy was leaning out of the door window, the rain running down his face and open collar. Byron smiled. Diehards. The railway attracted them by the hundreds; no matter what the weather they braved soot, smoke and rain to get the full experience of travelling on a proper railway. His grandsons were the same. So much better than many kids he encountered who sat in the carriage with their mobile phones, earphones jammed in their ears and could, for all they saw, be still in their bedrooms back home.

All the same, the next tunnel was a tight fit…

'Young man.' He raised his voice above the noise of the jostling, creaking carriages and the racket the wind was making.

Dad who was sipping a beer looked up at his voice but the lad was too lost in the rushing wind and lurching train to hear.

Byron turned to the father. 'Great to see him having fun,' he nodded towards the lad. 'But he'll need to pull his head in soon – the next tunnel is really tight.'

Obediently Dad left his pint and tugged his son's shoulder and the boy, his face glistening with rain, flopped down on a seat. He was about eight or nine with tousled hair which when dry would have been an interesting shade of rust. But wet it was dark brown. He fixed a pair of bright, hazel eyes on Byron.

'You can go back in a minute,' Byron assured him. 'But the next tunnel has only inches of clearance. I don't mind cleaning up a drop of rain, but squashed heads make a real mess – not to mention the paperwork.'

The boy inspected Byron's face and seeing the twinkle in his eye grinned back.

'You a policeman then?' he asked.

'How do you know that?' Byron demanded. The boy looked utterly unfazed. 'Dad gets the Ffestiniog mag; your picture's in it,' he said.

Dad looked as sheepish as the flock they had just chased off the track. 'Sorry… er, officer. I pointed you out to him on the way up. He's kinda hoping you might have to arrest someone.'

Byron contemplated his response. To say that he left police work behind when he was on volunteer duties would sound rather dull to the lad, but on the other hand he would be lying to pretend he missed it. Before he made up his mind the boy had a book open and was looking at him.

'What's a policeman say to his belly button?' he demanded.

'John, put the book away;' his Dad winced. 'Mr. Unsworth won't have time for your jokes now.'

Byron gave the dad a sly wink. 'Er, no idea,' he lied. This one was as old as the book the boy was clutching.

'You are under a vest!' the boy chortled triumphantly.

'Okay,' Byron shot back, 'why does a burglar wear blue gloves?'

John flipped the pages, but the joke book wasn't going to oblige him. 'Dunno,' he scowled.

'He didn't want to be caught red-handed.'

Mercifully Dad intervened. 'Tunnel's past now;' he gave his son a prod and he resumed his position at the window as the train descended the long curve around Llyn Mair. The lake, normally so enticing had a grey tinge from the rain-heavy sky.

'That was quite a delay,' the dad said, jerking his head back the way they had come. 'Were there a lot of sheep?'

'Must have been a whole flock.' Byron recalled the boiling, churning, woolly bodies stampeding around the tunnel cutting, bleating in blind panic as the stationary engine blocked their way. Usually it would be three, four, maybe five, but he had never seen so many of the stupid creatures strayed onto the track at once. The broken fence had clearly shown the means of their trespass but Byron suspected a rogue dog had panicked them against the wire and the posts had snapped. Typically it was at the top of the list for the trackway maintenance crew to inspect and repair the miles of fences this coming winter. They had finally driven the last of the animals back into the field and shored the broken posts to make a temporary repair. At the time the situation had alarmed him - sheep are heavy animals. Spooked sheep could trample you, especially in a confined space. So they had had to take their time, blocking the down track and herding them back up the bank and into the field. All the time the train had been stuck with the back half in Moelwyn tunnel. Even when the sheep were cleared they had needed to inspect the tunnel itself for any more beasts. By the time the driver and fireman were ready to go, the air around the locomotive was blue.

Byron had taken one last look over the fields before hopping back on the train. It was raining by then and the sheep were gazing guiltily through the murk. But there was no sign of any dogs.

'You a regular?' Byron knew the answer and for a few minutes chatted with the man whilst John hung out of the window until the train slowed to a halt in Tan y Bwlch.

The conversation improved his mood. Dad and son riding the trains and loving it. It was what made his weeks of freely given summer holiday time worthwhile.

'Tan y Bwlch!' Byron walked up the platform, bellowing to anyone who wanted to alight at the picturesque woodland station. 'Tan y Bwlch, ladies and gentlemen, anyone for Tan y Bwlch?'

A family clutching two sleeping children spilled out of the foremost carriages and dashed for the car park. A lady further back, unaware that the outward opening doors were routinely locked began to tug at the door handle in panic.

'Excuse me, the door's stuck!'

'It's locked, madam. Just move your hand and I'll let you out.' This happened more times than he could remember. He released her and walked up to the end of the train but no more passengers wanted to disembark. The open carriage, popular on hot summer days was predictably empty and the very last ancient green coach had only one inhabitant, an older man asleep in the far corner.

'Tan y Bwlch!' he called again, but he didn't stir. Byron glanced at the car park – all the cars were either going or gone. No point waking him up. Besides, he had seen this gentleman many times this week and he was staying somewhere in Porthmadog. Let him sleep.

This last carriage was a gem in the Ffestiniog collection – one of their earliest examples of rolling stock built for the company still in regular use. However it had no end doors so passengers in it were isolated from the corridor linking the rest of the train. He frequently warned families with young children that there was no access to the toilet.

With a last glance at the sleeping passenger, Byron waved to the driver and slung his bulk into the last covered carriage. With a sharp jerk, the train lunged over the bridge and into the cutting.

With typical Polish efficiency Marta had taken care of the refreshments so by the time they were heading down toward the lower woodlands he had a little time on his hands.

'Chris?' It was quiet back here, away from the engine and from experience he knew that he would have a good signal for quite some time.

Christine was his sister-in-law. 'Is Marlene able to speak?'

'I'll take the phone up to her. You having a good play?' He could visualise Christine heaving herself up the stairs to their bedroom. Opening the door and checking if his wife was awake…

'Yeah, pretty good. How's she been?'

'Ask her yourself,' Christine's voice dimmed a little then Marlene came on.

'Hi sweetheart.' He said.

'Wotcher plod. Nicked any fare dodgers yet?' She sounded grumpy. Byron sighed.

'You all right?'

'Me? Never better! I just love lying here watching daytime, evening and night time telly. Most of the detective shows are either so complicated real life couldn't make it happen or completely infantile. Do you know what? I'm missing work. I'm even missing the CPS evidence statement rubbish. Add to that another power cut and more expected next week.' She made it sound like his fault.

Things were bad, concluded Byron. Last year Marlene had been with him, albeit confined to a wheelchair and only able to carry out admin duties back in Porthmadog Harbour. But since then her crumbling spine had put paid to even that morsel of involvement. Following a protracted argument, this summer Byron had made the journey alone leaving his sister-in-law to manage an invalid, their home and two cats. Most evenings he managed to call her, but for the last few days he sensed she was finding it difficult to bottle up her frustration. He hoped her mood might improve tomorrow when she was hoping to get out of the house for a bit.

He missed her. No doubt about it. The years when they had taken a day off from volunteer duties and strapped their walking boots on to hike over the wilds between Tanygrisiau and the shoulder of Cnicht, admiring the different colours of the lakes cradled high up in the mountains and winding up exhausted in Beddgelert in time to catch the last train from Caernarfon. Unlike her sister as it was possible to get, Marlene had energy, a thirst to explore and a love of the area. A fast walker, she usually strode ahead of him past the multitudes of ruined slate houses and abandoned mine workings that had once brought huge wealth to the district, often first to the top of the ridge or leaping around playfully on a sheer ledge.

'Marlene, d'you have to do that?' he would protest. Unable to get to grips with his dislike of heights he refused her urging to bounce around with her on the rocky outcrops at the verge of some precipice. The height gave him physical pain in his guts, but Marlene was positively fearless.

Look at her now. Bedridden. The subject of regular visits by ever-changing health visitors. Her face on the pillow stretched with pain. Time and again the unfairness of it struck him – by comparison Christine would have taken to invalidity like a duck to water, but life chose her little sister, short, slim and active, to inflict its capricious will on.

'How are the meds making you feel?' He asked.

'Pretty rubbish,' she growled back. 'Steroids and more steroids. They got me into this and now they're supposed to help me. And you off gallivanting across the wilds with some nubile volunteer I bet...'

Her tone alarmed him. 'Look, I'll come back.' He tried to inject conviction in his voice.

'What and have me throw away this chance to make you feel bad? Not likely! Anyway, you've only a couple of weeks to go.'

'Then will you stop moaning you exasperating woman? Anyway, I've not had chance for a decent walk yet. Too much to do here.'

'You have my sincere sympathy. No, you stay there and have a wonderful time bossing unpaid skivvies around and drinking too much in Spooner's.... Charlie, GET DOWN!'

'Is that cat on the bed with you?'

''Course he is. Catching up on sleep.'

That was simply not possible. Charlie, their Tom cat would sleep twenty-five hours a day if he could. Marlene held the phone to the cat and the throbbing cement-mixer of a purr filled his ear. 'You know I don't like the cat in our bedroom.'

'Well you're not here, so tough. Anything exciting happen today?'

He told her of the lorry that had broken down on Britannia Terrace and blocked the Welsh Highland track for an hour and brought traffic tailbacks reminiscent of pre-bypass times to Porthmadog. He brought her up to date on the ongoing row about parking charges in the town car park. So many things to deal with on a busy tourist attraction many of which she made little comment upon. But she showed interest in the event that had just taken place.

'A whole flock of them? How many?'

'Darling, I didn't count them. It would put me off to sleep.'

'Yeah, very funny! But don't you think that's strange, love? Three, four, even half a dozen wandering on the line but a whole flock? Where was this?'

'Just as we came out of Moelwyn. Cutting was heaving with them. A fence had been flattened. Forty minutes by the time we were back underway.'

'I still think that's odd. Was it deliberate? D'you think someone was trying to rustle them?'

'Good luck to 'em if they were. They're the devil to catch. You'd be much better off going for lowland sheep in a pen.'

'Farmer might need to know.'

'He already does. We had his number in the van. We shored up the fence and he's going to repair it tomorrow. Hopefully that will be the last of it.'

'All the same…' Byron sensed Marlene was about to give him a task. He glanced at his watch. Three minutes to Penrhyn. She continued;

'Go and have a look. Use your DI nose. Tell me if anything seems wrong.'

'What could be wrong? Rheidol Railway trying to disrupt us? Sheep protesting against Hydro Electric schemes?'

'I would like to know,' she persisted. 'Please!'

'You're just bored,' he said, then realised how callous it sounded. 'Oh, I'm sorry, love, I didn't mean it like that.'

There was a long pause, then Marlene's voice came back, heavy with frustration. 'Yes, I'm bored. Sick and tired of being an invalid with no real chance of walking again…' Her voice choked. Byron paused, then asked;

'Seriously, do you want me back? The team would understand.'

Her tone softened. 'No love. You play trains. There's no point in both of us being stuck back here. Chrissie is good company, even if she wants to fatten me up for Christmas.'

'I heard that!' came in Chrissie's voice from somewhere.

'You were meant to!' Marlene shot back. 'Byron, love, do something for me, will you?'

'Anything.'

'You still got Monday off, yeah? Well walk from Tanny to Bedd, will you? Our walk. Eat your lunch on Cnicht, look out across the bay and I'll be there with you. Text me when you're at the top.'

'There's not usually a signal…'

'There will be. Gotta go. 'Bye love…' Byron could tell she was nearly crying. He felt a wave of glumness wash over him.

'Chin up, darling.'

The train whistle sounded the approach to Rhiw Goch. A mournful wail that rolled around the moist woodlands and blanketing cloud. Whoever designed that whistle knew their geography. The Maentwrog vale had changed little for centuries. Deep, ancient oak woodlands clinging for grim life to clefted rocky slopes with pockets of marshy ground feeding a multitude of tiny streams that hurled themselves into fast-flowing rivers racing to dilute the sea. Some fed dams and hydro-electric power stations along the way but their presence was no more than an interruption in their headlong progress. Isolated hamlets were sprinkled around the place; chapels converted to houses, small farms and garages. Higher up around Blaenau Ffestiniog, the grey piles of slate teetering precariously on the mountain slopes threatened to engulf the buildings below. The long, keening whistle gave voice to the brooding mountains eviscerated of their slate hearts, the mist-dripping trees, the wheeling kites, the sunlight glimmering on the distant estuary and the tangible sense of timeless grandeur. It was an old, achingly beautiful landscape but without Marlene it lost some of its appeal.

The train whistled again, summing up the melancholy Byron felt.

There were no passengers waiting at Penrhyn and only a handful wanting to alight at Minffordd. By the time the train was crossing the Cob some of the lost time had been recovered. None of the spectacular mountain peaks inland were visible and rain was lashing in from the sea driven by a wind that buffeted the carriages. Ahead, Moel y Gest was shrouded in murk. As they swayed to a halt at the harbour Byron went back along the train, checking windows and collecting the rubbish from the tables. He bumped into Marta in the buffet car. She saw the bag of waste he was holding.

'Thanks for doing that, Byron. Shall I do the doors?'

'You sure, Marta? You did them at Blaenau. Besides it's chucking it down out there.'

A brief quizzical look as she registered the unfamiliar English expression, then;

'No worries. We have rain in Poland too.'

Up ahead the fireman down on the tracks uncoupling the loco gave a soggy thumbs up to the driver and the engine, lightened of its load, sprang forward towards the coal bunkers at the end of the station. Once refuelled it would make its solitary way back across the cob to the workshops where the residual ash would be cleaned out and the engine spruced up for the start of another working week.

The rain was coming in horizontally, now. Byron shivered as he gathered his rosters together and glanced at his notebook. So much to do, but the weather forecast promised fine for much of Monday. He resolved that unless a dire emergency arose he would keep his promise to Marlene and take the day off for a long walk.

He shrugged his collar up against the rain but as he walked towards the station, cold tendrils of water crept down his neck. He shivered. The hog roast at Minffordd would be a grim affair tonight.

'Byron! Come back please!'

He spun round. Marta was running down the platform, her hair flapping in the wind and her steward's uniform blackening with the rain.

'What is it Marta?' She seemed breathless which was odd. Marta could and did run half-marathons for a pastime.

'P… please,' she choked, heaving great gasping breaths. 'You need to see this.'

He had to wipe the rain off his glasses to see to follow her slim figure as she led him back up the carriages. Past the standard class, the buffet, several more newer coaches, the gloss of their varnish deepened by the rain. Past the open wagon to the last carriage, the ancient green coach, smaller and squatter than its companions.

Marta hung back as Byron approached. The only open door was swinging in the wind; he had to catch it to avoid it slamming back on him as he peered inside the dark interior. He knew what he was about to see.

He had witnessed violent death many times. It is rarely dignified. Dead people don't feel discomfort. They don't care if they are wet or collapsed in an awkward posture. They don't care if their clothes are rucked up or they have broken limbs. They lie where they die.

The man he had seen asleep in the last carriage was not going to wake up. He had pitched sideways and slipped half-on, half-off the cushioned seat. The platform lamp shining through the window illuminated his outstretched right finger pointing accusingly at a small handgun at his feet. A pool of blood had collected beside his head and overflowed onto the floor.

Marta slumped against him, her shallow breaths rustling in his ear.

CHAPTER 2

SATURDAY EVENING WAS BAD ENOUGH; the first sound of sirens brought the drinkers out to stand in the wet and speculate about what was happening in the last carriage. The roving squad car had been quick to arrive and swathe crime scene barriers around lampposts and stationary coaches, but by Sunday the rubberneckers were thick on the ground. They pressed against the tape hoping for a glimpse of gore. Legitimate passengers trying to board the five past ten mingled with gawkers and tempers became frayed.

'How long will it take?' Justin, station manager on duty, wanted to know.

Byron shrugged, not because he felt unhelpful but because he simply didn't know. Different police regions had different ways of going about things. The body had been removed yesterday evening. Being on the scene, Byron was able to secure the immediate vicinity, collect witness details and make a start on the long, often tedious process towards establishing exactly what had taken place.

Had this been on his own patch in Somerset, then he would played the part of the crime-solving equivalent of a General Practitioner, able to call upon experts in finding, lifting and comparing fingerprints, crime scene analysts, psychological profiling specialists – not to mention the unsung heroes of the mortuary who would build up a picture of the last moments of the cadaver before them. Like a doctor confronted by an unwell patient DI Byron Unsworth would select his specialists to confirm or disabuse him of his conjectures about cause of death - the only substantial difference being that his patient was unable to assist him in his investigations. But this was North Wales and beyond the polite formalities, anything else was not his business.

Colleagues respected Byron's level-headed approach. He toyed with ideas but was ready to discard them if subsequent evidence undermined them. It was his strong point. He never fixated on a specific cause then selected his data to support that notion. No,

Byron was always ready to change his mind and it made him a first class detective. Moreover he used the same approach to interviewing suspects – although he avoided the word if possible. 'Suspect' had too many negative associations. His milder, although more wordy, 'individuals assisting with enquiries' summed up his strategy. He asked gentle questions, searched softly but once he uncovered duplicity would wear down the unfortunate individual 'assisting him' until a confession broke through their guilty shell. Even then, his placid temperament made the interviewee almost relieved to talk through their crimes with such a gentle, understanding policeman.

'It could be your lad or lass in that interview room,' he told many a colleague. 'Treat them accordingly.'

'You must have some idea,' Justin persisted. Byron glanced up at the Sunday morning sky – greyish white clouds harried by a landward breeze but beyond them the promise of a fine afternoon. He sighed. His chance of a good hike tomorrow was diminishing.

'You understand it's not my show?' he told Justin. 'I can't just barge in here and take over. I'm Avon and Somerset force. North Wales Police would take a dim view of my doing anything more than the necessary.'

Whether Justin believed him or not was unclear. He breathed heavily and went back to his morning coffee muttering.

How long Byron would remain at Avon and Somerset was open to question. Since Marlene's illness, he had gone part-time. Younger men and women with keener minds were eyeing his job and the commissioner was calling him in for 'friendly chats.' They were more friends than colleagues so Byron found his boss' inability to level with him galling. Make him a decent offer to reflect the years of unstinting service to law and order in the South-West and he would gladly go. In the meantime, the trains beckoned.

'Have you a moment, Sir?' A representative of the local constabulary was hurrying towards him. 'Superintendent Gwillim Ward, Sir. I understand you discovered the body?'

Not exactly, Byron corrected him. That dubious privilege had been Marta's, but he had come a close second. He had all the names and contact details of passengers on the last train including his own. The file was in his temporary office and he would fetch it just as soon as the ten o' five had departed. Gwillim looked flustered.

'Look, Sir…' he began.

'Call me Byron. Isn't this the land of poets and song?'

It wasn't clear if Gwillim cared or not. 'Byron; I'm here to ask a favour…'

'Ask away.'

It was an extraordinary request. North Wales Police were stretched to breaking point. The ill-feeling about the three proposed Hydro-Electric sites had ignited civil unrest for pretty well the entire length of the nation.

'We're stretched,' Gwillim groaned. 'All leave cancelled, the overtime is crucifying our budgets. Last thing we need is a crime team out here soaking up valuable men.'

'You have to admit, the opposition have a point,' Byron murmured. 'I would take grave exception to having my home under eighty feet of water to keep English lights on and English taps running.'

Superintendent Ward didn't let on whether he appreciated Byron's outlook. 'It's at breaking point. No, it went beyond breaking point some while back. I've every officer manning the thin blue line between civilisation and chaos. So this isn't the best timing…'

He broke off. Byron sighed.

'You're looking for me to wrap things up here?'

'I'll buy you a coffee… Sir.'

Byron leaned back and stirred his cappuccino as tourists began filtering into Spooners for late breakfast. He wished he'd waited now – Superintendent Ward would probably have bought him the full Welsh in his attempts to ingratiate himself. Half a guilty sugar went into the foaming mug. Marlene would never find out, he reassured himself.

'You'll do it then?'

'I didn't say that, did I? But if I said yes, what resources can you make available?'

'Anything!' Gwillim said too hastily, then added; 'within reason. We'll pay your expenses, you can use my office, Gwen Chambers, the station secretary, will look after you and DC Dylan Woods will assist you in whatever way you need… why the smile?'

Byron hastily removed the dreamy grin from his face. 'Just thinking how much Welsh people venerate their poets and songsters,' he admitted. Right out here in the sticks Dylan Thomas lives on.'

'Well he'll be in good company then,' said Gwillim, drily. 'I assume your parents were hoping for a poet when they named you?'

The truth, Byron explained was much more pedestrian. He had been born in an ambulance in Byron Street on the outskirts of Bristol. The rush-hour traffic had forced the driver to take to the side streets. His only regret was that the driver had not taken an earlier turning and he had arrived in Morse Street.

'You'll do it?' Gwillim leaned forward expectantly. 'I mean, if things quieten down we'll take over. And let's face it; it looks like suicide, so it shouldn't be too long.'

'Hell of a place to top yourself,' Byron mused, irritably. 'Okay, Gwillim, I'll give it my best.'

His hand was vigorously shaken, nearly upsetting his coffee. 'I'd better move,' Gwillim said, reaching for his jacket. 'There's a riot threatening in Welshpool tonight.'

Preferring to walk to the station, Byron stepped out into the sunshine and headed down the High Street. The Sunday morning traffic was light and he could clearly hear the bells of St. John's pealing out their call to the faithful. Halfway along the Main Street he glanced down Snowdon Street, the air sparkling clean after the evening rains. The terraced houses framed distant Cnicht Mountain, shaped like a knight's helmet. He recalled the numerous times he and Marlene had climbed up the ridge and surveyed the grand panorama of Madog's Port and the many square miles of farmland reclaimed from the sea by the construction of the Cob causeway. He had just spent a difficult half-hour explaining to the volunteer team he headed why they were about to be virtually leaderless. This Sunday was likely to be busy and Marta was looking a bit down.

'I'll deal with this as quickly as I can,' he assured them and beat a hasty retreat.

The Police station was nestled next to the Piano showroom and the supermarket. For a small station it had a fair-sized car park, although it was mostly empty. It looked like a smaller version of the shops that lined the street against which a flat roofed building had been shoved. Before he could ring the buzzer, the door flew open and a small, rotund woman shot out her hand.

'You'll be DI Unsworth?' she demanded. 'Glad we are to see you yer. Dylan's been on his own all morning what with these troubles and Dai's still off sick with his back or so he says. Come in lad; don't let me keep you from your work. You can use the office upstairs, it's a bit stuffy but Dylan doesn't seem to mind. Come you in now…'

All this was said without pause for breath. Byron soon found out that everything Gwen did came out in a hurry. She showed him to an upstairs office then flitted around, making tea, arranging biscuits on a plate and clearing files from a cabinet, all the time talking as though her mouth was connected to her feet by a set of gears. By the time ten minutes had elapsed, Byron had to call time.

'Gwen, love, could you find Constable Woods, please.' He knew Dylan was down in town because Gwillim had told him so. He didn't need Dylan as much as he needed a few moments' respite.

When Hurricane Gwen had blown herself into the adjacent office and was rattling on the phone to Dylan, Byron stretched himself then cracked his knuckles. He tried a biscuit – it was soft.

He had a tedious and potentially unpleasant task ahead of him, but there was someone he needed to call.

'Byron? Aren't they running the ten o' five? Or have they found another guard?'

'Better than that, I've got a nice little situation for you. Can you talk?'

'I'm headed out to the hairdressers, just as soon as Chrissie can unfold the chair and find the keys. What've you got for me?'

He told her.

'That was last night,' she remonstrated. 'Why wait until now to let me know?'

'It was really late by the time I'd got things sorted,' Byron defended himself. 'Anyway, it's most likely suicide.'

'Great!' she grumbled. 'Get me interested with a body in the end carriage then tell me he did himself in.'

'That's off the record,' he protested. 'We might find a better explanation.'

'You'd better, boyo. Every snippet, every shred, everything said, you tell your lovely wife and let her think it through.'

It was their standard, if questionable, procedure. Byron had long learned to respect Marlene's gift for spotting the anomaly in a set of circumstances. It might be a strange text message or an odd reaction from one of those assisting in enquiries. On the other hand it might be something so normal it seemed wrong. Unlike her husband, Marlene would obsess about the potential guilt of a suspect and challenge him to prove otherwise. Many times she had been proved wrong, many more her intuition had helped Unsworth nab his villain.

'Marta found the body?'

'She was doing the unlocking. Shook her up a bit.'

'Did she seem genuinely upset? Wish I'd been there, I could have gauged her reaction.'

'Now hold on!' Byron remonstrated, 'You're not suggesting Marta went down the train, letting people out and then calmly blew his brains out? On the platform with people all around?'

'I'm not suggesting anything yet, hang on…' Byron could hear her calling to her sister. 'Chrissie's ready to go, so just tell me as much as you know and I'll cogitate under the hair dryer.'

'There's not much yet. I don't know whether anything has gone off for ballistics or fingerprinting and how long it takes and I haven't had chance to interview anyone yet.'

'Who'll interview you? You are as much as a suspect as the rest.'

Byron shrugged at the phone. A lot of procedure was being ignored here. No one was expecting a crime. Whoever the man was in that last carriage and he still didn't have a name, he was being assigned a suicide's death. Which it most likely was.

When Constable Woods finally appeared it was with profuse apologies; 'There was a bit of a ruckus down at the mainline railway station, Sir. Few lads chucking bottles over the tracks. Sorry to have kept you waiting.'

Byron brushed the apology aside. 'What have you got for me so far?'

'I'll just get the file and personal effects, Sir. Wait you yer a moment.'

A file and a small plastic folder containing the few items found on the body were placed on the desk in front of him.

'I bagged a gun up, where did it go?'

'With fingerprints, Sir. Should be back somewhen.'

'More precisely?'

Woods flushed; 'Cardiff, Sir. It was couriered last night. I can phone in a bit for ballistics and see if they've had a shufti.'

Leaning back in his chair, Byron pretended to study the small collection of effects. In reality he covertly inspected his new colleague. PC Dylan Woods had a tall, rather gangly frame with a head that seemed just slightly too big. When he crossed his legs and leaned back in his chair, Byron caught a glimpse of an immense pair of feet, encased in regulation boots. First appearances did not favour PC Woods – he was the stereotypical flat footed PC Plod. But Superintendent Ward had spoken highly of him; very capable and resourceful and recently in line to be promoted to Trainee Detective Constable when funds allowed; there was more about PC Woods than the exterior suggested.

Woods had sandy coloured hair that was thinning at an alarming rate. He cracked his knuckles, the sound shockingly loud in the small room, then picked his teeth. It was a nervous tic that he repeated many times that morning.

'We'll download his phone calls when IT have unlocked it, Sir.' Woods ventured.

'Okay, that'll wait anyway. Let's start at the beginning. What was his name?'

'John Edward Coles. Born December 'fifty one, married with no children.'

That put him comfortably into retirement. Byron loosened his collar. 'Rather stuffy in here, any chance of a window being opened?'

'That I can,' said Woods, rising from his chair, 'but I warn you, by mid-morning the racket will be getting to you. Something about this place attracts the traffic noise.' He flung the window open and a waft of cool air crossed the office.

'Thank you. So what was done last night? After I finished up?'

'As I said, sent the gun off to Cardiff, body taken to Ysbyty Alltwen which is only round the corner – I can take you if you'd like…'

'No need, I know where the hospital is. I might do that later. What about his widow?'

'Informed yesterday evening. Lives in Leicester so should be here this afternoon. By the way, Sir, I've set you up a password so you can use all our computers and the like.'

Byron was beginning to warm towards him. 'Thank you Dylan. Now can I suggest something that might help us both? Let's get another cup of tea, see if Gwen can find some better biscuits and I'll tell you what I know. It'll help me to get it straight in my mind.'

When the sound of Gwen's voice had receded, Dylan got up and quietly closed the door. 'Can't be too careful, Sir. She's a good lass but it's her bingo night tonight and they'll be after any info they can winkle out of her.'

'My secretary back at HQ was just the opposite,' Byron chuckled. 'Everything was a state secret. How many days leave your senior staff may have left – no way would she tell you without a signed authorisation.' He cleared his throat, selected a biscuit and began.

He had seen John Coles several times in the last fortnight, travelling up and down the line. Getting on and off at different halts, with his rucksack, walking boots and telescopic hiking pole. A lean, wiry man with sandy unkempt hair framing a weatherbeaten intelligent face. Shaggy eyebrows above piercing brown eyes, sharp nose and a thin mouth. On his own, never waiting to see the train depart but striding purposefully up some mountain trail or off into the woods. He'd exchanged a few words with him, usually to confirm that he wanted the train to stop at Dduallt or Campbell's Platform. Yesterday he had checked Coles' ticket at Blaenau and asked if he needed any refreshments bringing to him. The answer had been negative. In a rare display of verbosity, Coles had produced a small hip flask and with a wry smile had said; 'As you can see, I have my own.'

Apart from the sheep on the line, the journey down had been uneventful.

Dylan paused from picking his teeth. 'But you say you looked in on him at Tan y Bwlch?'

Byron pondered the question. It was one of those situations where the lament, 'if only' sprang to mind. If only he had rapped on the glass to see if the sleeping man had woken up. Immediately the point of his decease could have been narrowed down to just half of the thirteen mile length of the line.

'I thought it best to let him lie,' he sighed. 'I knew he was staying in Port, and at that time I guessed he would be heading home so I let him sleep on. Those carriages rock you like a cradle. I have to keep busy or I nod off myself. Pity I didn't check, though.'

'No reason why you should, Sir. You don't look at every sleeping person and think; 'I'll just make sure he's not taken a bullet in the skull whilst my back's been turned.''

'All the same,' Byron grunted, 'I'll never hear the end of this; 'Senior detective fails to spot corpse,' or something like that.'

'He might really have been asleep,' Dylan ventured helpfully.

'If he was then we can rule out suicide.' Seeing Woods' bemused look he went on; 'if you were all set to end your life, would you take a refreshing nap just beforehand?'

'Now you put it like that, no.'

'So we have three questions; was it suicide, plain and simple, was it an accident with the weapon? Or was he done in by person or persons unknown. When can we expect some data? When are fingerprints due?'

'Local CID will be fingerprinting the carriage about now,' said Woods.

'Good luck with that. A few hundred people might have used that carriage this week, especially when it was sunny earlier on. Still we can at least exclude a few dozen staff and volunteers that I know were at Minffordd getting ready for the pig roast.'

Woods, returned to picking his teeth then replied;

'Of those three options, don't you think the accidental death is the easiest to rule out? Once ballistics have sent their report, we'll know how close the gun was to his head when the trigger was pulled. If he was cleaning it, it would have left little if any residue on his head.'

Byron agreed. Accidental death would be first to be dismissed once they had the report in. The trouble with criminals nowadays was that they knew all the tricks. They only had to watch the detective programs on telly to know to wear gloves and close fitting garments that wouldn't shed fibres, keep their hair tucked away, avoid speaking and check out CCTV beforehand so they wouldn't have their faces spotted.

'So let's put accidental death on the shelf for the moment,' he agreed. 'That leaves us suicide or something that is made to look like he took his own life.'

'Question, Sir,' said Woods.

'Fire away.'

'Don't you think it hinges on the gun? Whose was it? If it was his, then that would suggest he took it – deliberate aforethought and that sort of thing, and used it on himself.'

'Well we can answer that one now. Login to records, look for owners of registered firearms and see if he's on the list.'

'Sure thing.' In spite of his finger rummaging around his teeth, Woods quickly scanned the database. After a few minutes he shook his head. Byron felt a twinge of excitement. Marlene, he thought, you're going to be a happy girl...

'It was a small weapon, more for personal protection which suggests he was afraid of something.' Byron had trouble suppressing a smile. 'That's assuming it was his gun.'

'Hell of a place to murder someone,' Dylan objected. 'Doesn't suicide fit better? John Coles leaves wife, soon to be widow, takes himself off to his favourite walking region, does a number of walks then tired, happy and fulfilled ends it on a train.'

'I call that selfish,' Byron growled. 'Like jumpers who throw themselves in front of mainline trains. They don't get to see the poor sod who has to collect the body parts scattered along a mile or so of track. They don't have to look the driver in the eye as he throws up his lunch and goes off sick for a year. They don't see the thousands of passengers cooling their heels as the train cancellations stack up...'

'Of course, Sir.' Dylan Woods could see he had hit a nerve. 'But don't you think it would be like a compliment - you know, I could die happy up here?' Seeing the look on Byron's face he changed tack.

'But as you said, if it's murder, why make it look like a suicide? And why on a train?' He returned to fiddling with his molars and Byron reflected some more.

'It seems we have too little to go on at the moment,' he said. But let's assign actions to each of our three possibilities. One; if it's accidental…'

'Ballistics report,' Dylan replied. 'Should show gun some way from head, angle of entry unusual, that sort of thing.'

Byron nodded. 'And why did he have an unlicensed firearm? Two; it's suicide…'

'Reasons; financial statements, home life, any history of mental illness, medical records…'

'Top man! And the question of the firearm still applies. And thirdly…'

'Motive, means and opportunity.'

'You watch the detective soaps as well.'

'Taught me all I know, Sir. Where do you want me to start?'

'By closing that window.' The traffic noise was building up. Dylan banged it shut and sat down at the computer. Byron stood up and shoved the chair under his desk.

'I'm going to head to the hospital and take a look at John Coles in better light. So I suggest you dig around a bit, see what you can find.'

'Do you want to borrow a car, Sir?'

'No, the walk will do me good.'

Dylan bent over the screen, the top of his head showing through his wispy hair. Byron was uncomfortably aware how quickly the heat built up in this room.

'Do you have a secure laptop with roaming internet thingy?'

Dylan glanced up. 'Of course. Why?'

'I'd like to move to a different office this afternoon.'

It was just over a mile to Ysbyty Alltwen, perched high up on a bank near Tremadog with a fine view of Moel y Gest, the gentle mountain that presided over Porthmadog town. From the top of there you could see the coasts as far as Harlech and Tonfanau in the south and Pwllheli due west. On a clear day you could see the coast of Southern Ireland. Byron's feet itched to be in their boots, scrambling through the waist-high bracken instead of padding along hard, indifferent pavements bordering the main Caernarfon highway. It was only forty minutes to the top of Moel y Gest. He decided, he might nip up there instead of boozing at Spooner's this evening. Marlene would approve. Reluctantly he crossed the main road and headed up the drive to the hospital.

'Well that's accidental death out of the equation,' he murmured an hour later as he left the building. It was too soon to be confirmed - the autopsy was scheduled for five o' clock but the distinctive seared and visible blackening to the head wound on Coles' body told Byron that the muzzle of the gun had been pressed to his temple when it was discharged. The exit wound was not hideous, in keeping with the calibre of the revolver but death would have been instantaneous. The entrance wound was on Coles' right temple, the angle of the trajectory had taken it out of the other side above his left ear where it had lodged in the woodwork behind.

Had he been asleep when he had reached Tan y Bwlch? Possibly, but Byron doubted it. It would take a cool customer to sleep if he was in a suicidal frame of mind. So the likelihood was, embarrassingly, that Byron had not recognised a corpse. Not that it bothered him – he would be ribbed mercilessly about it, but the windows were smeary with rain, and unless he had physically opened the door, for which there had been no reason, the carriage could have been full of corpses for all he would have seen.

It seemed likely that Coles' disagreement with the handgun had not sent him flying off the seat. That figured, it was only a small weapon. But when Marta had discovered the body in Porthmadog, it had definitely fallen over sideways. He remembered the vicious jerk on leaving Tan y Bwlch – the driver letting in the regulator too quickly in his haste to make up time. That would have been enough to dislodge Coles from his upright position to lying sideways across the seat.

There was a bench in the hospital grounds overlooking the view of Moel y Gest. Pausing to buy a coffee and sandwich from the league of friends of the hospital, Byron sat down, ate his lunch and took out his phone.

'What've you got?' Marlene wasted no time in coming to the point. Byron told her.

'So it might not be suicide?'

'It might not be murder, either.'

''Course it is!'

'You sound very sure,' he chided her.

'I get this gut feeling,' she began. Byron groaned. 'No, you've got it too, I can tell. You're seeing something bigger than an unhappy man who tops himself on holiday.'

'The difference is,' he told her, 'I have to file a report based on something more than a bad feeling in my belly.'

'That's why you need me,' she responded sweetly. 'You do things by the book, I'll follow my instinct. May the best woman win.'

'Speak later, love.' Byron had spotted the police car sweeping up the drive. Dylan and a couple of female passengers. 'The widow has arrived.'

Mrs. Janice Coles walked briskly from the police car towards the main entrance of the hospital. She was slightly taller than average with a physique that suggested exercise, careful diet and attention to appearance. Her well-layered hair was only fleetingly flecked with grey; evidence that Mrs Coles was embarking upon old age on her own terms. Dylan lingered behind to help another female from the car – a much shorter and saggier person whom Byron soon found out to be a cousin. She, by contrast, looked appalled. When Dylan spotted him rising from the bench a look of visible relief washed across his face.

Byron intercepted Janice Coles just as she entered the porch of Ysbyty Alltwen.

'Mrs. Coles, I presume?'

She returned his gaze with little obvious interest. Then;

'Shall we just get on with it?' Her tone was not clipped or brusque, but neither did it betray the slightest wobble of a woman facing an unpleasant task. It was matter of fact. As was her reaction when ten minutes later the sheet covering the body of her husband was pulled back so she could inspect the face.

'Yes, that is John Coles. That is my husband. Thank you officer.'

'Would you like a few minutes, madam?' Byron murmured.

'No, but just allow me...' With that she bent over the still form and planted a light kiss on the pallid forehead. Contrasted with her apparent indifference it seemed a strange action.

'Mrs Coles,' Dylan rested his hand gently on her arm. 'Could you spare us a few minutes?'

'Can Katrina come with me?' Mrs Coles' cousin had remained in the hospital cafeteria whilst the unpleasant duty was being performed, which was just as well as she might had broken down sobbing. Dylan was no doubt afraid of this still happening so he said,

'We would prefer you on your own if you don't mind. It won't be long.'

Although they had made introductions of sorts in the entrance, Dylan went through the motions again as they settled into the interview room just down the corridor from the mortuary. Mrs Coles nodded briefly to both Police Officers and settled herself, back magnificently straight, and regarded them steadily.

'For the record, Mrs Coles,' Dylan said, producing a bulky folder and a small voice recorder that he placed on the table between them, 'you have formally identified the body to be that of John Edward Coles, your husband. Is that so?'

'Yes, that is, or was, my husband.'

'I will give you contact details for myself and my colleague, Byron Unsworth, should you need to ask for help in the next day or two, you know, when the body will be released so that you can finalise transport and funeral arrangements, that sort of…'

She cut him short. 'Yes, thank you.'

Byron was thumbing a leaflet that had slid out of the folder. It was a guide to the process of registering following a death in suspicious circumstances. He twitched it towards Dylan who slid it across the table.

'This will cover most of what you need to know, but would you like me to go through it first?'

Byron almost mouthed her reply; 'no thank you, that will not be necessary.'

'You understand that you cannot register your husband's death until the Coroner has completed his investigations which might take a day or two?'

'I was not aware but thank you for pointing it out.' She leaned forward slightly. 'When you contacted me yesterday, you said he had been shot. Did you apprehend the killer?'

'Madam, we are trying to establish whether your husband was killed or took his own life. My colleague, DI Byron Unsworth was present last night. He would like to ask a few questions. Do you feel able to help at the moment?'

Of course she could. She remained composed as Byron began the probing questions; had her husband been behaving unusually of late? Any moodiness or mental episodes? Did he use medication or had a diagnosis of some terminal illness? Was he prone to depression? Did he ever talk about ending his life?'

The answers came back without hesitation; no, no and no again.

The difficult questions he kept for last. How were their finances? Here at least he did detect a flicker of indecision.

'John dealt with that side of things,' she said after a pause. 'So I can't say. But you will doubtless check.'

Dylan filled the resulting pause. 'Did your husband have any enemies you know of?'

'Not that I am aware.'

'Any threats made?' he persisted.

And so it went on, her replies becoming shorter by degrees, finally amounting to little more than an arching of her eyebrows accompanied by nod or shake of her head and a soft release of breath. Something about her manner prompted Byron to ask;

'May I ask what your job was when you worked?'

'I was a mathematics teacher,' she said softly. Byron inwardly smiled. The teacher, marking a pile of homework books, seeing the stupidity inherent in her pupils and writing her caustic assessment of their dreadful work in sharp, red pen at the foot of the page. This current exercise was a waste of all their times.

'Forgive me, Janice, but one of the things I must ask is how things were between you and John. If you don't mind my saying, you don't…'

'Seem upset?' Janice Coles had a piercing gaze. Byron returned it mildly and waited.

'John and I had a long marriage, Officer. We have been together for just over fifty years, through good times and bad. And one of the things that made it work was that we kept out of each other's way for much of the time. It was the way we both wanted things. We didn't go out for candlelit meals at restaurants with outrageous prices; we didn't hold hands in public and not much in private. He took himself off for his long walks, I to my occupations. What he got up to or with whom, I did not enquire, neither did he tell me. But we always came back to each other. Yes, we shared things, but we gave each other plenty of space.'

She picked up the leaflet, twisted it between her fingers and Byron watched her.

'I will most likely shed tears for John if and when I feel the need to. But that won't be now, neither will I make a scene. It won't bring him back. So please respect my reactions. They are what he would expect.'

Byron nodded. 'Of course, madam.' He felt like his homework had been returned with the comment, '*could do better*' at the bottom. He was about to get up from the table when Dylan slid a bulky item from the folder.

'Do you recognise this?'

She stared at the gun and her lips snapped into a thin, red line.

'That thing? Is that what killed him?' she almost spat at last.

'You recognise it,' Dylan acknowledged. 'It was his gun?'

'If you look at the handle or whatever you call it, you will find ingrained red paint. It is all that is left of the initials DMC. Durban Mining Company. They gave that thing to him.'

'You knew about it then?'

'I told him to get rid of it!' Her composure had vanished. She was reddening with fury. 'He assured me he had. How dare he keep it?'

'Where did he get it?' Byron wanted to know, his voice soft in the quiet room.

In his job as a mining engineer, John Coles had spent months in South Africa. The mining complexes were vast areas employing many thousands of native and immigrant miners. Dangerous places to visit and senior European or American visitors were sometimes given a firearm for personal protection and tuition in their use.

'How come he brought it home? You are aware it is unlicensed?' Dylan asked.

She was indifferent towards its legal status. It was John's weapon and she had insisted it be dumped in one of the skips employed during Leicester Police force's firearms amnesties. He had assured her he had disposed of it. Shaken, now, she told them how, back in the seventies, John's employer had sent him to a mine in Durban. Things were already sour between the local workers and the immigrants but during his stay they turned rapidly worse and the company began to pull staff out. Many had fled, fearing for their lives. Those with weapons had kept them for insurance.

Nineteen seventies. Airport security was a pale imitation of what would be routinely expected now. A handgun stashed away in a suitcase could be kept at home, no one any the wiser.

'When did you last see it?' Dylan asked, but Janice Coles, her fury now bottled, became less cooperative and her replies lacking in any substance.

'I told him I never wanted to see it again,' was her final word on the matter.

'Well, that was a turn up for the books and no mistake.' Byron remained behind with Dylan as the widow stalked out towards the hospital entrance. 'How did you get the weapon?'

Dylan grinned. 'Came by courier just before I left. I have the ballistics and fingerprint report here though I haven't had time to glance at it yet. But never mind that, what do you make of the grieving widow?'

'What's your take on her?' Byron countered.

Dylan picked his teeth. 'She's a rum one, no mistake. Real cold fish if you ask me.'

Byron disagreed. 'I've seen all kind of grief,' he mused. 'Those who wail and weep right across to those who barely seem to care. There's no almanac on how to go about it. Her way is as legitimate as any other woman who finds that fifty years with the same man has just finished.'

'You believe her, then?'

'I'm not sure what there is to doubt. She could have put an act on, cried, snivelled, that sort of thing but it would look fake. What she did, even if it was cold, was genuine.'

The thought sent a shiver through Byron's large physique. If it was him in that mortuary, how would Marlene react? All their years together, their shared adventures, their idiotic times, their blazing rows, their tender moments. How would it appear in that moment of truth when one of them could no longer respond? Would the sum total of their lives together reduce to a dry kiss on the forehead? Thankfully Dylan interrupted his maudlin reflections.

'You'll change your tune if we find she's paid out ten grand to a hit man.'

'That I will,' Byron agreed. 'Have you had lunch?'

Dylan had eaten.

'Bring the laptop; we'll use my office this afternoon. I'll come back with you if there's room in the car for me.'

Sheila in the ticket office was watching out for Byron. Leaning towards the opening, she said,

'It's set up, Byron, like you asked. We've put a reservation on number eleven. You'll be wanting coffee and biscuits?'

'Thanks love. And do you have the footage?'

A DVD in a case was slid across the counter. 'All cameras, all day like you asked.'

He turned to go to the platform, but Sheila called him back.

'You still good for Wednesday evening?'

'I'll let you know.'

Dylan looked bemused as they climbed into carriage number eleven. One of the older types with locking doors, but access to the rest of the train. Byron stretched his big frame out and threw a few notes on the varnished table. Dylan was examining the map etched into the surface.

'They're bonkers about this outfit,' he murmured, tracing the black line that showed the twisting track of the railway and its stations set into the grain of the table.

'You just worked that out? Well bear that in mind when we look at this evidence. This is not just grown men and women playing trains. This is an obsession that grips people from an early age and doesn't let them go. You need to have that in your mind if you think that John Coles was motivated enough to end his life here.'

'Not sure I follow, Sir.'

'Nor am I, but what I think I'm saying is we will need a really good reason for suicide. Otherwise he'd have done himself in somewhere else.'

'Forgive me saying, Sir, but you're biased.'

'That I am,' Byron agreed as the guard blew his whistle and the train began clanking and squealing across the Cob towards the Boston Lodge workshops. 'That I am.'

CHAPTER 3

BYRON'S 'OFFICE' lumbered across the causeway. Dylan wanted to view the DVD of CCTV footage from yesterday straightaway, but Byron stalled him, preferring first to recap on what they knew. He threw windows wide open on both sides of the carriage but the air flow began lifting papers off the table so they had to half close them. As the train whistled around the bend, past the workshops and headed for the road tunnel he relaxed back against the seat cushion and addressed his new colleague.

'Accidental death;' he waved a finger in the air between them. 'You've seen the body; burns and gunshot residue at the entrance wound. Do you think we can rule it out?'

'I'm fairly sure.' Dylan agreed.

'So that leaves us with either self-inflicted or unlawful killing by person or persons unknown.' He lifted two fingers. 'Either way, victim was almost certainly dead before Tan y Bwlch. What does the fingerprint report say?'

Dylan logged into the laptop and found the file. 'Not much. A partial print which was a likely match to Coles was found on the barrel of the weapon. A couple of less well-defined ones around the butt and the trigger. Is that usual?'

Byron couldn't say. Fingerprints were rarely as obliging as the crime novels suggested. A person with dry skin might leave poor prints. No real help there.

'What about the fingerprints on the carriage?' Byron already knew the answer.

'Hundreds of good, bad and indifferent impressions on the handles, windows, frames, wooden interior and exterior. A good number were fuller impressions of the victim's prints obtained last night. But too many more partial or unidentifiable ones to be of use.'

Byron knew what Marlene would conjecture. She would say that a valid reason for staging a suicide in a public place was that the mess of conflicting data would make isolating the perpetrator's prints well-nigh impossible.

Ballistics report was hardly more helpful. The bullet recovered from the woodwork behind Coles' head was the only one that had been fired by the gun. One shot. They would have to wait for the formal analysis of the wound before confirming what they both already knew – the gun had been in contact with the skull when the trigger had been pulled.

The train was slowing to a halt at Minffordd. A few people waiting to get on tried opening the door handles, but had to wait for Paul, the guard on duty, to unlock the doors. Two men with a dog tried rattling the doors of Byron's 'office,' but were directed elsewhere.

Marta appeared in the doorway. 'Would you like a drink?' She looked drawn and pale.

'Marta!' Byron exclaimed, a little guiltily. He'd been meaning to check on her. 'Why are you working today? You'd do better to take a break.'

She dismissed the suggestion with an impatient click of her tongue. 'I need to keep busy.' Then, 'have you found out anything? About the dead man I mean?'

'Sorry, Marta,' Byron said firmly. 'I can't talk about it to anyone. But I would love a coffee.'

Dylan placed an order too and they went back to work. As the train creaked its way up to Penrhyndeudraeth and beyond, they skipped through sections of the CCTV footage on the DVD.

The train was just emerging from Moelwyn tunnel when Byron stretched himself and yawned. The footage was hardly scintillating stuff. A montage of the camera feeds from Harbour station, Blaenau and a few cameras along the way installed to counter the acts of vandalism that erupted from time to time. People came and went, climbed on and off trains and milled around taking photographs of the locomotives and their families. They spotted Coles boarding the ten o' five from Harbour. He walked to the front of the train and settled himself next to the buffet. The next time he appeared was alighting at Tanygrisiau where he marched off towards the Lakeside café without waiting for the train to depart. With boots, rucksack and a waterproof coat he looked every inch the veteran hiker.

'Wonder where he went,' said Byron before allowing his gaze to wander to the lake they were passing on the right. The lake formed the bottom pond of a peak storage hydroelectric plant. During the night countless thousands of gallons of water were pumped up the mountain to the top lake nestling behind the Stwlan Dam, three hundred metres above them. Then as demand kicked in for the morning breakfast and kettles were clicked on, electric hobs heated and a multitude of other electronic devices made their grab for power, the system would reverse and the water would surge back down the pipes buried deep underground and turn the pumps, now acting as generators, to supply massive amounts of power to the grid within less than a minute.

The bottom pond acted as an indicator of demand on the system – if it was low it meant that water was up in Stwlan Lake at the top of the mountains so demand was low. If high, water was barrelling back down, turning the mighty turbines, then demand was great. The longer the demand the higher the pond level. The original railway track, built long before the power station, had been flooded by the installation. If the water level was low, it was possible to walk along the derelict track bed almost to the flooded tunnel. After a high power demand the water crept up the slight incline of the old track and submerged it several times a day.

The water was so high now it was lapping at the long grass that normally formed the verge of the lake banks. National demand was exceeding supply as usual and the Ffestiniog Pumped Storage system was trying to make up the shortfall. Byron recalled a conversation with his brother in law who worked as a power systems consultant. Over a pint they had discussed the creaking National Grid. The demise of the coal and gas fired power stations had been forced by environmental legislation but had taken place too soon for nuclear generation to plug the gap in demand. The nearest generating nuke in Somerset was still five years off, Wylfa C in Anglesey eight years before it came on stream. In the meantime the public and industry used electricity like it was going out of fashion.

'When the nukes come on stream, we'll be okay?' Byron had asked his relation.

'Not at present capacity, and environmental groups make it so difficult to build new ones. Don't bother freezing your food, Byron,' Paul had replied ominously. He was referring to the loss Byron and Marlene had suffered to their store of frozen food during the last winter's power outages.

Renewable energy did its valiant best to supply the serious shortfall, but it was spasmodic. Wind was plentiful in Wales but sunshine notoriously fickle so electricity surged often at times when demand was low. Peak storage stations like Ffestiniog soaked up some of this unwanted power but there were only a few of them. So the thrust of government energy policy had shifted back to hydroelectric schemes. Several deep valleys situated in the heart of mid-Wales, well served with rivers, had been proposed as sites to the fury of their inhabitants and Superintendent Gwillim Ward had now to deploy his men to keep the peace.

Byron remembered the time when a constant supply of electricity was a given. It was always there, cheap and ready to serve them. But last winter and much of the spring had seen power rationing because of shortages across Europe. The lights had gone off and stayed off for many long hours in regions of southern and mid-England, apart from London and the south east who seemed to be a special case. It was a new experience for many who were too young to remember the industrial unrest of the nineteen seventies.

'There he is.' Dylan had found their man.

John Coles strode briskly into the field of one of the cameras at Blaenau Ffestiniog station, his rucksack swung over one shoulder. He used the station toilet then reappeared as the locomotive detached and ran round to be refilled with water. He seemed to dither, looking at different places to sit before waiting for the end carriage doors to be unlocked. Part of the reason for this, Byron noticed, was that the reservation signs which had blocked off many carriages on the way up were still in place. Marta should have removed them as soon as the train arrived in Blaenau. Not that it mattered, there were only a few passengers waiting to board and she was busy anyway unlocking carriages for passengers to alight or embark.

'How's he seem to you?' Byron asked Dylan.

Dylan shrugged very unprofessionally. 'Not sure what I'm looking for?'

'I mean, does he look uneasy, edgy…?'

'Not really. But you can't get much detail on these recordings. Ah!' His back straightened. 'Now there's a dodgy character if ever I saw one!'

Byron thought his colleague was being serious until he recognised himself, in guard's uniform marshalling the few passengers on that late service into the carriages. Glancing at his watch, then a quick word with the driver who was just finishing his tea off and a swift check that all the doors were closed before the train shuddered forward in its last down trip of the day.

'Dodgy my foot!' He snorted. 'Fine, upstanding figure of a man if you ask me.' But Dylan wasn't listening.

'Have we got another camera feed? This is all down the wrong end.'

There were two or three that monitored the station. The system recorded them all simultaneously with the option of playback in split screen or single screen. The playback was rewound to when Coles appeared, the second feed selected and they watched Marta unlock the door, then he clambered into the end carriage. Then Byron, in his capacity as guard checked his ticket and exchanged a few words with him. As Byron had recalled, Coles showed him his hip flask as he declined refreshments on that journey. Thereafter he settled back, stretching his calf muscles.

Byron found his attention wandering. It was all so normal. Too normal. Within an hour or so this man would be slumped lifeless in the corner seat. He didn't look on edge or like a man about to end his life. Not that it was a deciding factor. Sometimes those who had made the decision to end their life were calm – they had done all their agonising so it only remained for them to make the last moves to finish it. They were resigned.

'Does he look resigned?' Byron pondered out loud. But Dylan had seen something else. With less than a minute before the train left a man and a woman with two young children, barely more than toddlers hove into view. They were late and approaching from town had lighted on the nearest carriage, the last carriage. By now, Marta had locked the doors but seeing them she hurried up the platform to them.

'What d'you make of that?' Dylan wanted to know. Now it was Byron's turn to shrug. There was certainly an innocent explanation, but seen from the CCTV it seemed slightly bizarre. There was a short, animated conversation watched by Coles from within the carriage, then the family were led further down the train and admitted near the front.

'Why not just let them in there?' Asked Dylan as the train moved away, leaving swirling eddies of steam and smoke in its wake.

'I'll ask her,' Byron said.

The first station, Tanygrisiau, had a single fixed camera which gave them a brief glimpse of Coles partaking of his 'refreshment' in the last carriage. Lolling against the rear of the coach with his hip flask in his hand. Byron thought again; *'too relaxed. Much too at ease.'* But this was his gut feeling. What was he expecting to see? Their man cleaning his gun? Marlene might have a feeding frenzy on these observations but a coroner would take a dim view of speculation like this.

The mobile phone records, financial statements and the hundred and one other transactions that ordinary people left as they went through life – like social fingerprints - would need teasing out of the bank accounts and service providers to see if anything smelled bad. That would lie ahead of them in the next few days. Boring, sometimes unpleasantly intrusive, work to see if John Coles was as commonplace as he seemed.

By the time their train had stopped at Blaenau, they had viewed a bit more CCTV footage but it was uninspiring.

'Would you like some cake?' Marta popped her head round the door. 'Sandy's birthday yesterday, we've still got some here.'

'Sorry Marlene,' Byron thought as he took a slice laden with butter icing. Then as Marta turned to go he called her back.

'Could you spare us a moment?' He watched her face. Her skin was quite pale anyway, but he noticed she lost a little more colour.

'To do with yesterday?' She said faintly.

'Do you feel up to just giving us a hand?'

'Sure thing.'

Whilst Dylan rewound the camera footage, Byron nibbled pieces off his cake.

'This bit,' Dylan pointed to the screen. 'We're a bit puzzled why you didn't let them into the carriage.'

'Oh that!' Marta looked relieved. 'They had infants. I explained to them that there was no getting to the rest of the train so if the little ones needed the toilet they...' She broke off. 'Was that the right thing?'

Byron assured her it was and Marta left to open doors.

'She was the one who found him,' Dylan guessed. 'Marta what?'

'Kowalczyk. One of those surnames you can never pronounce. Too many consonants,' he glanced at Dylan slyly. 'Bit like Welsh if you ask me.'

Dylan didn't rise to the bait. On the contrary he elaborated on a theory that the Welsh language was the product of a bad set of Scrabble letters. He looked back along the corridor.

'She seems upset.'

'I think it's rattled her more than she realises.' Byron resolved to spend some time with Marta later. She was a bit of a loner. In the two weeks she had been with them he had found her extremely hard working, committed to whatever task in hand and ready to take the initiative but she found communication difficult. There was a boyfriend somewhere out there and he suspected it wasn't a happy relationship but he had not pried into her private life. She was, he also realised, very pretty in a plaintive kind of way. Had she grown up in a place with a good dental service, her teeth could now have been straight and her smile dazzling.

As the train began its downward journey, they ran through the rest of the DVD. Nothing sprang out at them, not even the camera feed at Porthmadog where the wall mounted cameras managed to miss the end of the train. Flashing ambulance and police car lights, people hurrying around; all the trappings of a good tragic happenstance.

'Well that's that,' said Byron. 'Let's leave this at the station and I'll take another look through later.'

As they were pulling into Tanygrisiau, Byron remembered Marlene's advice. He had good shoes on and the day was turning pleasantly warm.

'Finance,' he instructed his colleague. 'Bank statements, transactions, you know what to look for. Then, if you have time, medical records. I'm going to take a walk from here. I'll pick up the next train down at Tan y Bwlch.'

'What're you looking for?'

'I'll let you know if I find it. If I don't I'm still on holiday, remember?'

There were two stops on the Ffestiniog Railway that impressed him with the contrast between when the train was present and when it had departed. The noise, the hiss of escaping steam, the sounds of humanity nestled together in a small space – all this filled the air when he alighted from the train either here at Tanygrisiau or even more so at Dduallt halt. But when the train clattered away, an almost palpable silence descended on the station. The blanketing quietness, perforated only by the distant cry of a curlew or the gossiping bleats of the ubiquitous sheep was something Byron looked forward to. It felt as if he had disembarked in an earlier, ancient time and modernity had retreated over the horizon.

The locomotive whistled its mournful warning and the road sirens struck up their keening duet as the train trundled over the level crossing, then silence began in earnest.

It took him twenty-five minutes to reach the rise through which the modern Moelwyn tunnel had been cut and a further five to reach the far end. There was a battered Land Rover parked at a rakish angle with fence posts sticking out of the open back and heavy duty wire fencing unrolled along the grass. A few sheep were watching with interest, no doubt looking for weaknesses in the completed job.

'You must be Mark!' He called to a middle aged man who was striking a fencing shovel into the stony ground.

'That I would.' Mark wiped the soil from his hands and straightened up. 'Was it you called me last night?'

Byron nodded. 'What do you think happened?' He indicated the broken fence posts scattered around the pasture.

Mark had no real idea. He picked up one of the old posts. 'These have been yer for a few years, but they had some life left in them yet. But they're broken clean off. Yer you go, take a look.'

The post had indeed broken off just above soil level. The wood was slightly rotten on the windward side where it was exposed to the incoming rain, but three quarters of it was sound timber.

'How many broke off?'

'Three. I think they crushed up yer against this middle one and once that snapped the fence pulled the other two in and down. Then all the silly things went over the bank yer.' He waved his hand towards the trampled brambles and numerous round, black droppings that showed where they had slithered around in the cutting.

'Are they all accounted for?'

'Far as I can see. Rustlers would've taken as many as they could.' Mark wiped his hands and leaned on his shovel. 'Yer you had a spot of bother down at the Harbour? What was that then?'

Unfortunately investigations were underway so aside from the barest details Byron could say nothing. Mark shrugged, trying to look as if he didn't care and returned to digging the old post stumps out.

'Mind if I have a nose around?' Byron asked.

'Feel you free.'

The trouble was, Byron reflected after twenty minutes of prodding around the long tunnel and adjoining moorland he had no idea what he was looking for. He was only doing it to please Marlene. He bid farewell to the farmer and walked onwards for another ten minutes to reach the loop at Dduallt. The path to Tan y Bwlch lay ahead, under the upward bridge, but just off to his left was the viewpoint at the top of the spiral.

'Where are you?' Marlene demanded.

'Dduallt viewpoint,' he told her. 'Want an update?'

'Is the Pope Catholic?'

It always helped talking to Marlene. Her keen mind would spot any inconsistency in a set of circumstances so it forced him to order his recollections into a tidy account before relating them to her. Sure enough she was soon asking the same questions he had.

'Did this John Coles seem jumpy on the CCTV?'

It would have been so easy to say that he had been and let her draw the lazy conclusion. But he loved and respected Marlene too much to do that.

'No, he seemed quite relaxed.'

'So not about to top himself then?'

They reviewed the investigations of the day. Surprisingly she had no issue with the cold widow.

'If it was you,' she assured him, much to his dismay, 'I wouldn't howl. I'd have too much to think about.'

'Thanks,' he grumbled.

'Any time,' she said after an awkward pause. 'You think he did himself in?'

'So far most things point that way. The weapon was his, his wife asked him to get rid of it, he obviously didn't. Only prints on it were his; barrel pressed against his head – classic suicide position. No one else in there with him, favourite place to end his life… when we get finance and medical something might come to light.'

'Wouldn't someone have heard the gunshot?'

'Perhaps they did, but he was right at the back and those trains clatter and bang a lot. Who'd think it was a shot? It was only a small weapon. We've got the contact details of all who were riding that train, someone might recall something.'

'Powder residue on his fingers?'

'That'll be for the Coroner to look at. They've got a roving forensic team who'll be called in if they need it.'

'Who saw him alive last?'

'Not sure; either me or Marta…'

'Ah!' She said acidly. 'The ever helpful Marta.'

'What do you mean?'

There was a pause. Then; 'she does seem to get everywhere. Extra shifts, doing the dirty work, sooo obliging.'

Byron sighed. Marlene got like this now and then. The new secretary or female investigator at work - if she was only half decent looking Marlene would conjecture that they were on the man-hunt and her overweight, semi-retired husband was a perfect catch. Or worse, she would accuse him of flirting. The problem was, if he made the slightest attempt to ridicule the idea, it only looked like he was hiding something.

'Marta's hard-working,' he said firmly, trying to sound reassuring. 'She's no family over here and I think she finds making friends difficult so volunteers for extra shifts. She does have a boyfriend though.'

Whether the last snippet of information appeased her, he couldn't be sure. But Marta had only mentioned him once. Was he in the UK or back in Poland? He made a mental note to pry.

'How is she today?'

'On edge. It's not every day you find a person with a hole in their head where one shouldn't be. We set up our office on the one-thirty. You'll be pleased to know I looked at where the sheep invaded the line.'

'And..?'

'Nothing much to see. The fence posts look as if something heavy pushed against them. Farmer didn't seem that bothered though. Anyway, that's hardly top priority now.'

'Mmm..!' Marlene murmured. 'So if there are no medical issues or financial irregularities we're still going to be saying he did for himself and leave it at that?'

'What else would you have me do?'

'I don't know. But I've said before, if it's too good to be true, it's not.'

'Yeah,' Byron agreed, 'you have a point.'

After she rang off he had plenty of time to wander onwards through the gnarled and twisted oak woodlands that flanked the Maentwrog valley. The path rose and fell steeply and was occasionally blocked by a massive fallen tree limb, mossy and flecked with semi-round fungi that looked like someone had hammered dinner plates into the wood. He thought he was still in good condition for his age, but by the time he turned away from Llyn Mair and had climbed up to the station he was sweating freely. The café was about to close but Ellie, manning the tea urn, made them both a coffee and found some rich fruit cake that needed using up and he chatted to her until the ten to six came round the corner. Having a few minutes whilst the train was unloading, he rang Dylan.

'Anything to report?'

'Medical records is normal, Sir. No debilitating diseases or dementia onset. Nothing like that. Hope I'm as fit when I get to his age.'

'Did you get chance to speak to his GP?'

'Very briefly. Quite shocked he was. Felt that if there'd been ought amiss he would have known.'

'Bank accounts?' Byron had a numb feeling that this was going to be the same.

'Hardly got started on them. But Dai Young will be back from sick tomorrow so it'll give me a bit more time.'

'Dai Young?'

'Sorry, David Young, Sir.'

'Unfortunate choice of name,' Byron remarked, grinning.

'Appropriate, though. Always something wrong with that one. Hypochondriac.'

'I see. When are you taking your weekend days? Can Dai… David cover for you?'

'What's a weekend?' Dylan asked. 'Out yer, we grab our time off when we can which right now isn't very often. And the other half keeps nagging me about getting the wood burner installed before it starts getting parky.'

Dylan lived in a terraced house in Prenteg. Last winter's power cuts had left them huddled together looking at a useless electric fire. Since then Dylan had acquired a rusty old stove and was in the process of refurbishing and installing it to supply hot water and radiators to their house.

Byron made sympathetic noises, but he knew that Dylan Woods was making a packet on extra shifts. He would cope.

'Bring me up to date tomorrow,' he instructed and rang off.

CHAPTER 4

THIS EVENING was a splendid contrast to Saturday's dismal arrival in Porthmadog. It was as though the weather had anticipated the tragedy then and was making amends tonight. There were over two hours of daylight still left and the sky, although lacking its earlier brightness, was clear apart from long bands of cloud stretched across it. They caught the evening sun and lit up like multi-coloured ribbons. Ahead, Moel y Gest Mountain basked in the warm breeze. Byron's mind was made up. He had his walking boots in the office at the station. A quick meal at Spooners followed by a brisk walk to the top to enjoy the view.

When he entered the station restaurant, his eye was drawn to Marta, alone at one of the far tables. Conscious of Marlene's remarks he considered sitting in one of the snug seats and pretending he had not seen her. Two things changed his mind; firstly it felt like an overreaction. Marlene was being irrational - Marta was a woman young enough to be his daughter. Besides which she would see him when he went to the bar to order his food. The second thing was that, as he approached, Marta looked up and it would have seemed curious indeed if he had not sat down with her.

Nevertheless he observed the customary politeness. No, the seat was free and yes, she would like him to join her.

She accepted his offer of a drink, choosing a glass of house white. She had been inspecting the menu and was ready to order so Byron added a small chicken burger (out of deference to Marlene) and returned with the drinks.

They made small talk; issues of the day's train services, problems which had arisen and how best to deal with them. But Marta made little attempt to conceal her misery.

'You all right?' He asked at length, taking a sip of his ale.

If she had been an English girl, she would probably have protested that she was fine, happy and healthy. But Marta came from a different culture.

'I feel frightened,' she mumbled.

This was an unexpected choice of words. 'Frightened? Why. Has someone said something to you?'

'No, Byron, but I keep seeing him there, fallen over on the seat. Who did this? Why?'

'Hold on, Marta. No one did this, at least not that we know. What makes you think otherwise?'

'You mean he killed himself? But that's awful!'

'Marta, it happens, now and then a man or woman reaches the end of a road. They cannot go on. I'm not saying I think it's right, but I've never been in their shoes.'

She inspected him; a pair of huge, grey eyes framed by smooth, clear skin in an oval face. He thought she was assimilating this profound statement until she murmured,

'In his shoes…?'

'I mean you need to be in their situation,' he clarified. 'Seeing and feeling what they do, we call it walking in their shoes.'

'Oh. And Mr. Coles, he had, as you say, reached the end of his road?'

It was in Byron's mind to repeat his earlier rebuff; to politely but firmly remind her it was police business. But there was a beguiling vulnerability about Marta Kowalczyk, a stranger in a strange land of mists and faeries, dragons and mountains and seemingly half faerie herself. If he felt like an intruder into this mediaeval region – how must she feel, a foreigner alone and now haunted by a violent death?

'It happens, Marta. Thankfully not that often but it happens.'

'Then he's an evil man!' she burst out, her eyes wide and fixed on him.

Byron almost spilled his drink. 'Steady on!' he hissed. Spooner's bar was still quiet and several heads turned. 'You think suicide is that bad?'

The bar tender arrived with their meal and she lowered her eyes, unwrapping the knife and fork from the napkin. Byron felt relieved

– it gave him a few moments to think. He fetched some tomato sauce and dipped a chip in it.

'I'm guessing back home they don't approve of taking your own life?' he ventured after a minute or two.

'It's a terrible thing to do;' aware of the notice she attracted earlier she spoke with a low voice, but a tense, rapid delivery. 'To destroy the gift of life. Such a cowardly thing. Few people will come to your burial; the church cannot bury you in consecrated soil. People will talk about your family, whisper behind their backs. They are the family of a *samobójstwo.* Disgusting, contemptible.'

Unable to think of an answer, Byron took a mouthful of ale.

'So if you think Mr. Coles did… committed suicide,' she went on, 'I would like to know the reason.'

'I am keeping an open mind, sorry, I mean I have not decided yet. Would you prefer he was murdered?'

She dismissed the idea with a flick of her fingers. 'No one should die alone like that. But what could make him kill himself?'

'That's what we're looking for. We check their medical records. How would you feel if we found he had an incurable disease and he had only weeks to live? Would you despise him then?'

'Has he?' She shot back.

'No, but there are plenty of good reasons why he could have topped… sorry, killed himself. He might have had money troubles.'

'He has a wife?' Marta drank half of her glass of wine in one gulp.

Byron sighed inwardly. If his intuition was right, Janice Coles was the one good reason John might have discharged a bullet into his brain. Prim was the wrong word. Prim suggested a show, an exterior of formality that might conceal a private mischievousness. Prim people could relax, let their hair down, even throw a custard pie if the occasion demanded it. But Janice Coles was frozen. He tried to imagine coming home to Marlene if she was like that. No fun, no spontaneity. Just coldness. But all the time he would be hoping and praying for the thaw, for her to show affection and love.

Year by year, the permafrost settling lower in the soil of their lives until... well until the dry, chaste kiss on his cold forehead sealed the end of their marriage. It was warm in the bar, the air filled with the noise of cheerful holidaymakers relaxing on an evening. But Byron shivered.

'He has a wife?' Marta repeated. 'She loved him?'

She saw the answer in the look on Byron's face.

'Can you think what it would be like to be married to someone who was showed no affection?' he said finally.

'But in Poland, when we marry we show dignity. We walk in the village side by side and people say, 'there's *Pan Kowalczyk* and his lovely wife.' We do not always hold hands. But when the door closes behind us we are...' she flushed appealingly and lowered her gaze again.

Byron loosened his collar. 'That's what we would call reserve, Marta. But I don't think Mr. Coles had anything to look forward to when the doors were closed.'

A silence fell between them. Her head was bent over her food. Her hair was a silvery blonde; it fell to just below her slim, shapely shoulders. Byron took the opportunity to eat his chicken burger and finish his chips with the salad. As he scraped the remains of the tomato sauce with the last of his chips he inspected Marta. She seemed to have calmed down. Good, he could get his scramble up Moel y Gest in after all.

'How was your food?' he enquired to the top of her head.

She looked up, tears pouring down her face.

'You are not minding?' she sniffed for the third time.

'No, it will do you good. It will do both of us good to get some exercise. I'm sorry I didn't get chance to talk to you sooner.'

In spite of Marlene's earlier comments, Byron had invited Marta to accompany him up the mountain. She had on sensible trainers and the ground underfoot was fairly dry in spite of yesterday's downpour. She positively snatched at the opportunity and Byron realised that she was lonelier than he had thought. As a rule, Ffestiniog volunteers were a rowdy lot, keen to muck in, quick to make friends around a shared passion. But now and then the rule failed and Byron felt a sense of responsibility to her.

'Sorry, Marlene,' he muttered as he hauled on his faithful, comfortable walking boots.

There were two well-used routes up the mountain. Byron chose the town side footpath which rose steeply from the road serving the industrial estate. Being on the sunless side of the hill the woods cast a gloom over them both. He would be glad when they rose above the tree line and into the evening light. He made small talk as they scrambled up the steep path, criss-crossed with tree roots but his companion did not seem keen to talk. Once she slipped on a loose stone and grabbed his arm.

'Whoa, careful,' he cautioned, noticing that she clutched him for much longer than was necessary.

Moel y Gest rose steeply at first, but once out of the woods, the path climbed more steadily through waist-high bracken, becoming boulder-strewn higher up. Byron pointed off to their left.

'See that path there? That's the other way down. It goes through the caravan park and down to Borth y Gest. My digs are in Borth y Gest.'

What were digs, she wanted to know. Byron explained, confessing that his days of staying at the Minffordd volunteers' lodge were behind him. It was too noisy and the beds hard. He preferred Gwyneth Williams' more comfortable Bed and Breakfast hostelry with her excellent breakfast and evening fruit cake.

'If we go down that way, through the camp site, we can pick up my car, and I'll drop you back at Minffordd,' he told her.

'Thank you,' she said, clearly struggling to keep her composure. 'You are a good man. I'm sorry about earlier.'

'You must understand, we're looking at all the possible options,' Byron said, brushing aside overhanging bracken fronds.

'It's still early days. We might find someone with a good reason to want him dead.'

'You have spoken to his wife. What did she think?'

Byron shrugged. 'She didn't think he had upset anyone enough to want to kill him.'

'But if she despised him, wouldn't she try to protect that person?'

'It's possible,' Byron conceded, 'but I didn't get that feeling talking to her. They didn't have a fulfilling marriage, but she hardly came across as a killer or even an accessory to a crime. I don't think she had anything to hide.'

They ploughed on up the rough path until the top came in sight. Byron explained that the highest point was off to their right but it was some walk and not much more elevated than where they now stood. To all intents and purposes they had climbed Moel y Gest. She seemed content with this concession and followed Byron to the rocky outcrop that gave the most spectacular views over the estuary and extensive coast line.

'That's Harlech castle,' he pointed to the craggy building in the near distance. 'Round the next headland is Barmouth and the huge, wooden railway bridge. It's a lovely place. You should explore the area if you have time.'

As he spoke he was aware that she was standing very close to him. Closer than someone who had agreed to a companionable walk would stand. She wasn't exactly pressed up against him, but she was well inside his personal space.

'Where's that over there?' she asked, pointing off to their right.

'Pwllheli,' he said, gazing out at the tongue of land jutting out into the Irish Sea. 'On a clear day you can see Ireland.'

All the time he was struggling with his confusion. Not just confusion, but guilt. What was he doing up here with this young woman who was evidently lonely, probably still in shock? What possessed him to allow himself to be placed in this compromising position?

Ahead, the sun was about to plunge into the sea. The sky was on fire; warm colours close to the horizon giving way to purple and blueish black behind them. Marta stood facing the sea, a slight breeze lifting the ends of her hair.

'It's so very lovely,' she murmured, her hand reaching around his arm.

'I'm reading too much into this,' thought Byron, looking dumbly at both of her hands, now clasped around his arm. She reaches out to me as a friend. Why shouldn't she? His daughter did the same if they went on a walk. But Marta wasn't his daughter….

A feeling of possessiveness began to creep up on him. She was consciously or otherwise appealing to his vanity – a younger and reasonably good-looking woman demonstrating that Byron Unsworth still had what it took. He mentally shook himself – there was an expression for this, one he had used many times of older men who fell for the blandishments of the younger, vulnerable female.

'Don't make a steaming idiot of yourself, Byron,' he whispered under his breath.

Then she placed her lips on the side of his face and kissed him. Lightly at first but moving herself around to face him. Her eyes were looking directly into his.

'Byron, don't be a fool!' But how to extricate himself? Then inspiration struck.

'You said you had a boyfriend?' He kept his tone light, even and measured, as if he was just making a passing enquiry.

It broke the spell. She unclasped his arm, moved back and stretched herself, heaving a big sigh as she did so.

'Tell me on the way down. We've not got much light left.' Byron turned and struck back towards the path. 'I get the feeling there's a long story here.'

It wasn't that long. She had met Huw Davies when he was backpacking across Europe. His easy charm and lilting Welsh accent had captivated her. He told her of his homeland, of the rolling hills of the South; the remote moors and peat bogs of central Wales and the towering mountains and steep-sided valleys of the North. He told her how he was captivated with her beauty and a lot of things besides. Being a poet and musician, he was able to earn his keep by playing his guitar and singing to entertain tourists wherever he needed a room for the night. Marta had kept him company for a glorious summer last year and they parted with the promise of meeting again. A promise he broke in keeping with the plots of most of the Celtic folklore he sang about.

'But you came expecting to meet Huw here? No, this way…' Byron placed a hand on her arm and directed her towards the path that led down to the campsite. With relief, tinged with disappointment he noted that this time she did not respond to his touch. *'There's no fool like an old fool,'* he reminded himself.

Yes, it had been the plan that they would meet up to work for a fortnight on the railway where Huw had volunteered in previous years, then backpack around Wales. Only when she was installed and half-way through her first week did his cowardly text come through. Marta punctuated her account with some short, explosive Polish words that needed no translation.

'But you stayed?' Byron asked as they stumbled down the rough path where it met the rolling green lawns of the campsite.

'Huw was right about this land;' in the gloom Byron glimpsed her crooked smile. 'It is special. I wanted to stay, to see more of it.'

They walked on, an awkward silence growing between them. Byron said finally;

'I'm always around if you want to talk,' He tried to sound detached but inwardly cursed himself. It was a perfect setting for something stupid to happen. His wife was bedridden, and he was alone with this strange, unearthly woman, cast up like a lost thing on the shores of North Wales and the two of them were picking their way through the cool, moss-scented eerie half-light of the campsite drive where it emerged onto the road. It was as though he had stepped back forty-five years; once more a giddy, love-stricken teenager grappling with the onslaught of puberty. *'Enough!'* he chided himself.

'I came to find you earlier,' she said, a slight tone of reproach in her voice. But your colleague said you got off at Tanny.'

'I needed to check something,' Byron hustled her across the lane. Lads from the campsites down at Black Rock used this road as a racetrack and he wanted to get down to Borth y Gest before it was really dark.

'Oh! What?'

'Why the sheep got onto the line by the tunnel.'

'They're always getting on to the line. That's what you told me.'

'In twos or threes, sometimes half a dozen. But not a whole flock. Someone was mucking around and it cost us a lot of time.'

'You're saying it was deliberate?' Marta sounded startled.

'This wasn't a gap in the fence, Marta. A big section of the fence had been pushed over.'

'Perhaps they broke it down themselves.'

Byron found the connecting footpath and they struck off across the dark fields. From the shadows sheep watched them impassively, greyish blobs against the hedgerow.

'I don't think so. The posts were still sound. Probably vandals but I need to ask around, see if anyone saw anything.'

Marta was quiet as they approached the top streets of Borth y Gest. His car was down on the sea front and by the time they reached it she seemed preoccupied. Other than small talk, very little was said as he drove her back through town then on to Minffordd where the volunteer hostel was lit up with the flickering flames of the hog roast.

'Ah, the great social event,' he smiled, easing the car across the rails and into the car park. 'I believe it was meant to be last night but they managed to postpone it. Well, here's your chance to enjoy yourself.'

She looked blankly at him in the dim light of the car interior. He tried again.

'Go on, mingle a bit. There're some great people here this year. And I know I shouldn't say it, but Paul Handley, the guard on this morning's service keeps asking about you.'

She shook her head. Byron felt a flash of irritation. 'Come on, Marta. You can't just mope around feeling sorry for yourself. Huw stood you up. Move on. I know for a fact Paul can sing and play the piano.'

'Are you staying?'

Byron shook his head. 'It's been a very long day. My landlady serves me a decent cup of tea and excellent fruit cake. I won't want to miss that. But you go and enjoy yourself. I'll see you in the morning.'

'Thank you, Byron.' In a swift movement she leaned across and kissed him on the side of his face. Then she was gone.

Gwyneth Williams had almost given him up for lost by the time Byron let himself in. 'I was about to put the cake away,' she chided him. 'No matter, I can boil the kettle. Would you like Earl Grey?'

She always asked and Byron's reply was always the same;

'That would be perfect.'

'Your wife rang,' she remarked as she brought the drink and cake in. 'About an hour ago. Been trying to ring your mobile, she has.'

With a guilty start Byron checked his phone. The battery was exhausted. So was he. He sighed. 'Can I use your phone?' he asked.

''Course, love,' she said and left.

Normally he would have valued another bout of verbal sparring with Marlene. She would be sitting in the armchair, popping painkillers and ruminating on the information she already had. But he felt a little bit uneasy. Unless he kept his voice light and cheerful she would detect he was feeling flat and want to know why. How could he explain his evening with Marta on Moel y Gest? He had been naïve and a little bit foolish. A cold thought crossed his mind - Marta could make allegations – but he quickly dismissed the idea. She didn't seem the type.

'She just needed a friend,' he murmured, pouring his tea and dialling home. Sure enough, after just the barest preliminaries Marlene asked;

'You okay?'

'Yeah, fine. Why?'

'You sound a bit, well, down. Where've you been? I've been ringing and ringing.'

'Sorry, my mobile was out of battery. I've been taking the air on Moel y Gest, trying to work out why John Coles would top himself.'

'You think that's what happened?'

'I'm open to alternatives.'

He answered her questions but he had already discussed this with Marta and didn't want to go through it all again. He began to get irritated and Marlene with unerring accuracy picked it up.

'I'll ring tomorrow when you're in a better mood.'

'Sorry, sweetheart, it's been a long day.' He faked a yawn.

'If you say so, but one thing to think about;'

'Go on...'

'To my mind, if it's murder, it's as close to a perfect murder as you can get. Means and opportunity – well could it be that those sheep were chased on to the line for a reason? You said yourself, many more than would normally stray...'

'I agree, that was certainly deliberate, but are you suggesting it was timed to stop the train?'

'Yep. Whilst you're faffing around down the front, knee-deep in sheep, Coles is at the back, all on his own. Like everyone else on that train, he pulls the window down, someone steps out of the darkness and, bang!'

'Someone who knew he had a gun? Someone who knew he was alone? You're running away with this!'

'I am not!' Now Marlene sounded cross. 'I'm just trying to deal with what I see. You see suicide, but there's a few things wrong with that theory.'

'Such as?'

'He was too calm, that's what you said. Topping himself on a passenger train, that's weird. If he loved walking so much, why not climb a high mountain then do it at the top? And where's the note. Have you found one?'

'Why is suicide on a passenger train weird?'

'Not so much weird, as incredibly convenient. It's a heavily used area. Thousands of prints. What chance of isolating those of whoever did it? As I said, means and opportunity. You go find the motive.'

'Okay, I'll throw the idea to Dylan tomorrow.'

'You'll do more than that. You'll go back to Moelwyn Tunnel, look for anything around where that last carriage was. Now go and get your beauty sleep.'

CHAPTER 5

BYRON SLEPT uncharacteristically late the following morning. He had to hurry through Mrs Williams' morning attempts to boost his blood cholesterol and decanted his coffee into a flask to take with him. He gave Jason, the acting team manager at Ffestiniog a quick ring to check he was up to speed with the day's agenda then drove to the station. He endured Gwen's greeting which was much ado about nothing, ordered some biscuits and eased himself into his office chair. Dylan was already bent over his screen, finger wedged in his teeth.

'What you got for me, Dylan boyo?' It was a passable attempt at a Welsh twang.

'Motive,' Dylan replied, running his finger down the screen.

'Motive for what?'

'I'll flip the file over.' Dylan pressed send and the file popped up on Byron's screen.

He cast his seasoned eye over the list of financial assets of the late John Edward Coles. It was a depressingly familiar story – a series of pension investments that had gone sour, leading to a dwindling lump sum and a re-mortgaged property. Poor interest rates had returned low yields and whether Janice Coles was aware or not, they were living on economic borrowed time.

'There's a good enough reason to do yourself in.' Dylan said.

Byron mused over this latest snippet. Marlene's words were still fresh in his mind. This was too good. Too text book. What she was proposing, though, had its own deep-seated problems. If the train had been stopped for the purpose of killing John Coles, how did the perpetrator get hold of the victim's gun to fire the single shot that ended his life? How did they know he would be alone in that last carriage? And wasn't the carriage window closed when he saw Coles at Tan y Bwlch? He scribbled a few notes to himself.

'Sir;' Dylan interrupted his thoughts. 'Don't want to get beyond myself right now, but, well, I've had the Super on my back.'

'Gwillim? What's he after?'

Dylan shuffled and picked his teeth agitatedly. 'To be honest, a quick finish, Sir. He's kinda stretched right now and wants me off this and back in the firing line. You know, the demos.'

'You don't sound eager to go.'

'I'm not. It's a rubbish call to man the barricades when it's your mates throwing the bottles at you. Trouble is, I kinda see why they're upset.'

Byron regarded his junior intently. 'So conflict of interest?'

'Absolutely. How would you feel if where you lived was going to be a lake?'

'I come from Chew Valley,' Byron smiled wryly. 'Heard of it? It's got a massive man-made lake built to supply water to the Bristol area.'

'That's not the same.' The speaker was in the doorway. Byron swung round. Gwen had a file in her hand. 'It's a disgrace. The reservoirs created here, know where the water goes?' Without waiting for an answer; 'Birmingham, the Midlands, England.' The last word came out almost as a snarl. 'The electricity; you'd think we'd have lower rates being as we had to lose the land to build the dams. Do we? Not a chance! Not even guaranteed supply. They generate it here, but we're first to see the lights go out. What d'you make of that?'

'Seems a little unfair,' Byron said, hoping to placate her. But Gwen was on a rant. 'We need to generate more power. That's what they say. More megawhatevers. Why? Why the sudden need for more?'

'Lack of generating capacity?' said Byron, mildly. She banged the biscuits down on the desk.

'Go to London. Place is lit up night and day. Lights burning, no effort made to turn them off. When I was young my mam used to clout me round the ear if I so much as left my bedroom light on.'

'So did mine,' Byron offered.

'Now look at the things; electric cars needing charging, computers, automatic lights that turn on day and night – no one wants to do the obvious.' She glared at Byron as if it was all his fault. 'D'you want to know what that is?'

'You're going to tell me anyway.' Byron was getting annoyed and Dylan looked uneasily from one to the other.

'Turn things off. Then we won't have to have windmills cluttering up the hillsides; we don't have to have our farms flooded and turfed out of our homes to make way. Doesn't take much to....'

'I seem to recall the Welsh Assembly approved the Dam sites,' Byron's tone was acid. He felt uncomfortable. Wales was like a second home to him and Marlene, but now they were taking the rap for big decisions made high up in the echelons of power.

'Bunch of traitors,' Gwen snorted. 'Few backhanders from Westminster and they queue up like sheep for the slaughter.'

'Gwen, do us a favour, will you love?' Dylan, too, had had enough. 'Can you check through these statements from the people on Sunday's train? Ring them up. Background checks, any criminal records, you know the sort of thing.' He thrust a sheaf of papers at her and bundled her out the door.

'Sorry about that, Sir. She's a good lass, but she gets it going now and then.'

Byron waved the apology aside. 'I know she won't believe it, but I largely agree with her. Whatever the answer to the energy shortfall, flooding more of this lovely land won't help matters. And yes, we do waste power like we waste water.' As he said it, he thought guiltily about their garden sprinkler back home probably just turning itself off.

'I'll have a word,' Dylan said. 'She's no right to rant at you like that.'

'No, leave it. All the same we'll use my office later if you don't mind.'

Dylan's eyes lit up. 'Yeah? Good by me.'

In spite of his irritation, Byron smiled inwardly. Another potential convert to steam railways.

As they waited for the train to pull away from the station, Byron found himself musing about where this was going. The case was already closing. They needed the autopsy report, forensic analysis of the injury and confirmation of what he already knew. Coles' mobile was with them, awaiting an unlocking code. He would chase Dylan for that. If that didn't provide any contrary indications, he would direct Dylan to start heading towards a verdict of suicide. Marlene wouldn't like it, but she couldn't win every time.

Phil Braithewaite was driving today. He knew this because the train moved smoothly away. Phil treated his engines, in his own words, with the care of a gentle lover.

Another train started in his mind. It was one he returned to often. Detective work was hyped by movies beyond all recognition. Sherlock only had to see some commonplace object marginally removed from its customary or expected place, or a person behaving ever so slightly abnormally and his brilliant mind would deduce a sequence of events that led to the villain. It was good, entertaining stuff, but he found the suppositions irritating. It conjectured an orderly, tidy world where people did predictable things in response to stimuli. Cause and effect. So if you could observe peoples' habits closely enough, any deviation thereafter would be a sure indicator that they were involved in a fiendish crime. QED.

But this was not the world he knew. Thirty-five years in the force taught him that people on a personal scale were inherently unpredictable. They did things that you could not anticipate in a hundred years. They didn't smoke the same brand of cigarettes every day, or drink the same beverage. They broke with routine often, but sometimes with spectacular results. Yes, come to think last night he had been intending to have a pint of the local Porthmadog brew, but unexpectedly he had changed his mind. Why? Because he could. He wasn't a machine. Most people put coats on in cold weather. But sometimes he took his off and savoured the prickly cold on his bare arms. Why? Because he could.

Byron watched the low wall of the Cob speeding past. Why was he thinking like this at this moment? Was it not the years of experience speaking? John Coles' past and personal effects might or might not throw light on the situation, but he wasn't going to expect everything to be neat and tidy when they closed the case. John Coles had been a human being – erratic, impulsive and subject to whim. If everything didn't make sense, it was because not often did everything make sense. Disconcertingly sometimes people like John Coles took their own life because they could.

Phil was driving the locomotive pulling this train, of that he was sure. But he had to allow for the possibility it might not be Phil but someone else driving with uncharacteristic care.

'This come through, Sir.' Dylan thrust the laptop on the table in front of them.

Byron skimmed the formal autopsy report. Single bullet, small arms, corresponding to the one carried by the victim. Gunshot residue and searing of the entry wound. The muzzle had been pressed to the skin. Massive tissue trauma leading to instantaneous death, yada, yada.

But the one thing standing out was the comment by the forensic analyst who had accompanied the autopsy. Coles was right handed – they had seen that from the CCTV footage of him. But there was much less powder residue on his right hand than would be expected. And none worth speaking of on his left. Make of that what you will.

As the train, loaded with two huge coach excursion parties and a number of last minute shows lumbered up the incline that would rise steadily for the next twelve miles, Byron returned to his train of thought. People were unpredictable. His marriage to Marlene was a case in point. When she had been transferred to CID and assigned to his team, she had had every red-blooded male in the building practically drooling over her in a very unprofessional manner. She was twenty-five then with long, very dark hair, a figure to kill for and soft dark eyes that could beguile the unwary into thinking she was a soft touch. She was pretty, clever and being petite made her even more alluring and she knew it, so it was no surprise when she was practically engaged to the son of the district Police Commissioner – a bright, easy-mannered lad with aspirations, connections and not a little money to hand.

When Marlene Fox broke off that relationship and took up with the relatively unknown slightly pudgy Detective Constable Unsworth who was often, much to his annoyance, mistakenly called 'Brian,' it was unkindly rumoured that the lovely Marlene was on the rebound and marking time. Marlene and Byron just didn't make sense. Mind you, it didn't make much sense to Byron at the time who still remembered spitting his coffee into her lap when she first reached out to hold his hand.

The Minffordd cemetery trundled past. Mostly simple headstones peppered with the occasional ornate monstrosity. His mind flicked back to Marta, striding ahead of him up Moel y Gest in her shorts. She had lovely legs too…

He broke off from his reverie. Dylan was on the phone to someone. From the one-sided conversation it appeared that Dai with the bad back was back from sick and in the police station. Dylan off-loaded some tasks onto him and then sat waiting expectantly.

'How do you feel about the Hydro-electric proposals?' He asked him, more for something to say.

'Don't like it, if truth be known,' Dylan shrugged. 'But no one would deny we need the power. This country always supplied the raw materials. Look at the iron, and the coal we dug out of the ground. The slate mines – why this town supplied the world once. Just another call on us, really.'

'Talking of mines, Coles was a mining consultant. Any idea what one of them does?'

Dylan picked his teeth. 'I'd be guessing, but there's plenty of people up here could tell you. I'll ask around. Wouldn't mind betting he came here in a professional capacity before he retired.'

This was an interesting notion to Byron who filed it away for future enquiry. It made sense. The place was still host to several working mines and John Coles might have known and been known by miners and their bosses.

He was about to embark on a review of what they knew for certain when Marta popped her head around the door. She looked a little agitated still; maybe she was embarrassed about last night.

'Would you like drinks? I'm not serving but I can bring you some specially, if you like.'

They would like. As she was going, Byron called her back.

'When we stop at Tan y Bwlch, could you have a word with the driver? Tell him to stop just short of the Moelwyn Tunnel. I need to have a look around.'

'I will do that,' she said and left.

'She looks rough,' Dylan remarked, his gaze following her retreating figure.

'Give her time,' Byron replied. 'She's had more of a shock than I realised.'

They sat in silence for many minutes, watching the lowlands trundle past. Then Dylan spoke.

'Are you going to tell me about the tunnel? This'll be your second visit. Is it anything to do with the case?'

Byron considered stalling his colleague. In light of this latest material regarding Coles' financial state, any theories involving killers emerging out of the darkness of Moelwyn Tunnel to gun down a respectable, retired professional seemed fanciful to say the least. Word spread around, and he didn't want his own division to get wind that DI Unsworth was letting his imagination run wild. But looking at Dylan; boyish, lanky, with huge feet and slightly too large head, he conceded that neither of them really had much credulity to lose. So, sparing the full extent of his conjectures he outlined his reasons for revisiting the site. He was gratified that Dylan didn't flinch at the idea.

'It would be a bold move, Sir,' he mused. 'And it would certainly give us plenty to think about.'

'Go on…'

'Well, Sir.' Dylan paused to bite his thumbnail then went on; 'It's not a killing any more is it? It's an assassination. And that begs a motive. What was Coles doing that made it necessary for him to be killed with all this effort to make it look self-inflicted? Then there's the business of the gun. I can't see Coles handing it across for someone to shoot him with it. So…'

'So ..?' Marta appeared in the carriage doorway with coffees and some cake. Byron tried to signal him to hold his thought there but he went on;

'Well it means that they knew he had a gun, took it from him beforehand and shot him with it to make it look like he did it to himself.'

'You should be married to Marlene,' Byron thought. 'Those for us, Marta? Thanks.' He took the tray from her.

'I'll speak to Phil in a minute,' she said and flitted away to unlock the train doors for Tan y Bwlch.

'See if you can think of any useful lines of enquiry we can pursue to prove this,' he said to Dylan. 'But I warn you, if word gets out we'll both be a laughingstock.'

'No, I'll say I was acting under your orders, Sir,' Dylan smiled engagingly. 'But I'll ask around. Usual stuff in the movies…' he ignored Byron's wince, 'the victim is useful because of his work. So first thing when we get back to Port, I'll find out what he really did.'

'I'm going to recommend you for accelerated training,' Byron said to himself. *'You're too bright to be stuck out here.'*

'Any news on the mobile yet?' he asked. Dylan tapped away at the laptop. After a couple of minutes he said; 'Still waiting on IT, Sir. They're a bit snowed under. I'll have a word with Charlie, see what I can do.'

Dylan was like a spider at the centre of a vast web of contacts; people owing him favours and some shadier of the great unwashed on whom he relied on for information. Getting a mobile password was easy enough for him. Byron moved on.

'Has Coles any convictions?'

'Nothing to speak of. Except for motoring violations. He's currently on a ban which will end at Christmas. Too heavy on the gas pedal from what I can see.'

'Ah!' Byron exclaimed. 'Hence the need to use trains to get to where he wanted to walk to and from. Makes sense. Where was he staying? I'm guessing no car means he was local to Porthmadog.'

'Correct,' Dylan said after a few more keystrokes. 'Travelodge on Penamswer Road. Know where it is?'

Byron did, but his experience of chain hotels didn't auger well. Too many staff coming and going. Still, someone might remember something. 'Give it a try,' he advised.

'Better than that, I'll get Dai Young down there. Lazy git could use a walk out.' He picked up his phone and after a rapid-fire exchange of banter had sent Dai on his way with instructions not to return until he had spoken to as many staff as possible.

'I'm getting off at the tunnel, and I'm going to ask around if anyone saw Coles on Sunday. Last known movements, that sort of thing.'

Dylan favoured him with a dumb grin. 'Only thing up there is sheep. Can you talk to them?'

'Stupid boy! I'll ask around Tanygrisiau. See if anyone saw anything. But for that gem, I'm giving you a little job when you get back.'

Dylan looked suitably chastened when Byron instructed him to visit Janice Coles and see how up to date she was with their financial state.

'The Black Widow;' he chewed his thumbnail. 'Just what the doctor ordered.'

'Watch her reactions; see if she is genuinely taken by surprise. Perhaps she'll appreciate your sense of humour as well.'

CHAPTER 6

BYRON LEFT his colleague pretending to grumble, but clearly enjoying his free train rides. In the short time he had known him; he had come to value his laid-back but capable approach to the problem before them. He caught a glimpse of Marta watching him from the buffet car as the train pulled away and waved but she didn't respond.

As before, once the train had clanked and heaved itself into the darkness of Moelwyn tunnel and beyond, the blanketing sense of silence descended around him. It was at once comforting and disquieting. It brought calmness to him, away from the relative chaos and noise of Porthmadog but he also found it unsettling. A silence that seemed to say, *'you don't belong here. Here is where the warrior warlords and druids belong. Men as hardy as the rocks and women as fierce as the winter streams.'*

He had a torch this time and worked his way slowly through the long tunnel. Its walls were coated with a cement rendering, but water ran through crevices and down the walls to join the rivulets that slobbered along the soakaways either side of the oily track. There were slippery sheep droppings squashed on the sleepers and tufts of wool fluttered on the brambles alongside the repaired fence. One or two sheep inspected him suspiciously.

'Come on,' he said, looking into their inquisitive faces. 'You saw what happened here. Don't make me have to take you in for questioning.'

A short distance in from the far end, where the last carriage had been he turned his flashlight on the ballast.

After ten minutes he exited into bright sunshine. He was no Red Indian but he could see there had been activity around this end of Moelwyn. A few dislodged ballast stones, showing lighter shades of grey. The sheep hadn't got up this far, so it had to be human activity. Trouble was, human activity wasn't difficult to come by here. Maintenance crews worked regularly, keeping the drains clear, checking the tracks, cutting back the overhanging vegetation. Kids sometimes foolishly ventured into its dark interior. Tomorrow this area would be alive with anoraks taking part in the Gravity Slate Carriage run. How much easier it would be if he found a spent bullet casing except that the gun used on Coles retained them.

'Hello grumpy.' Marlene said, her voice cautious. 'Found anything?'

'You don't even know where I am,' he complained.

'Oh, I do. You're sitting on a wall, just above Moelwyn wondering how to admit to me I'm right.'

'Yes, yes and no. You're right about location, I am sitting on a rock not a wall but I'll let that count, but no, it's not looking hopeful for your theory.'

Marlene listened in silence as he related the parlous state of Coles' financial affairs.

'You think that would push him over the edge?'

'I think like most people, denied a loving relationship, he turned to money. Lot of travel, lot of spending to compensate. When that began to dry up, what was left?'

She pondered this assessment, then;

'So any evidence of activity round the tunnel.'

'Few hundred spent shell cases, few hand grenades, couple of corpses, but nothing much else.'

'Oh shut up!'

'Sorry, sweetheart.'

'If you think I'm going to drop it just like that, you're wrong.'

'I'm not,' Byron said with conviction. 'I'm open to you piecing together a watertight case for unlawful killing. But I'm not promising to buy it. For a start, how did they get the gun off him?'

'Got a few minutes?'

Byron settled himself back on the warm rock; in his rucksack was the flask with the breakfast coffee. It was still warm. He poured himself a drink and listened to his oracle.

'You're making assumptions,' she began. 'No don't interrupt. Coles has a gun. But does that mean he carried it all the time? It could have been back in his hotel room.'

'Got that covered. Or Dai Young has. He's questioning the staff at his hotel.'

'Who on earth is Dai Young? No, never mind. You need to know if there was any suspicious activity, a break in or some such.'

'I'll let you know when Mr Young reports back.'

'Please do. So here's one suggested scenario; Coles leaves the gun tucked away in his case in his hotel room…'

'How do they know he has a gun anyway?'

'I'm coming to that, don't interrupt or I'll talk to the cat instead. Coles doesn't take his gun out into the wilds because he feels no need to. He's not expecting trouble, but he's curious about something. He never turned the gun in. Why? I think he felt the need for it at other times.'

She paused. Byron tentatively said; 'You're implying Coles was an agent? A mercenary?'

'No, I'm just saying that when he retired from whatever he did in South Africa he didn't stop entirely. Hence the travel. Mining is a funny business. All sorts of less than legitimate sides to it, like blood diamonds, illegal extraction, that sort of thing. So he would keep the gun and they knew that he would. With me so far?'

Byron nodded and she continued.

'Sunday morning, Coles checks into Harbour station. He has an annual railway pass?'

'Yes, just renewed it a week or so back.'

She paused. 'Really? Oh good! He boards the first train, the ten o' five and gets off at Tanny. Where does he go then? Not a linear hike, like across to Beddgelert or he wouldn't have been on the last train back. So a circular walk. We've done a few around there; the Slate village, Cnicht…'

'If he went over Cnicht he'd probably descend on the back road to Croesor and come back to Tan y Bwlch.'

'Exactly! So we can discount that route. Could he have done Moelwyn Mawr, Moelwyn Bach and round the dam? Anyway, that's not the main issue. He arrives back at Blaenau. Strange because he could have just waited for the train at Tanny, but he walked on. Why?'

'Go on,' Byron prompted, realising for the umpteenth time why he loved this woman.

'I don't know. Could be he had an eye on the weather and came down early. When did the rain start?'

'About six.'

'Hmm. Well, anyway, he didn't go as far as expected and decided to walk along to Blaenau to meet the train there. Let's face it, Tanny's hardly got much in the way of comfort once Lakeside Café is closed.'

'It could be he went across Craig Nyth and down into town,' Byron suggested.

'In which case, ask around. See if anyone saw him leave and in which direction.'

'I was about to do that, you exasperating woman. It's my very next task.'

'After lunch at Lakeside?'

'Okay, you know me too well. So run the rest past me.'

Coles boarded the train; she explained, parked himself in the last carriage and the assassins rounded up the sheep, smashed down the fence and drove them into the track. A few sheep would not do - the train would only slow down and chase them along the track, so it had to be a whole flock. Once the train was halted, they would wait in the dark until the occupant of the last carriage dropped open the window. The shot would be loud in the confined space but the bleating of the frantic sheep much louder. Coles would slump back into the seat, the gun placed in his hand and his fingers pressed around the butt and then it would be dropped to the floor.

'Have I covered everything?' she enquired, trying to hide the note of triumph in her voice.

'Almost. So are you suggesting Coles knows who killed him? He's dealt with them and let them know he's armed?'

'Something like that. Something to do with mining, but not legal.'

'This is an assassination, then.'

'Sounding increasingly like it. I might be wrong about motive – could be drugs...'

'He didn't seem the type.'

'Whatever he was doing, it was of sufficient importance to make killing him necessary. But it had to be made to look like suicide. Which suggests that... oh damn!'

'What's up?'

'Power's off... again. Look, I'll talk later. But do me a favour will you?'

''Course, my love.'

'Find out how much was left in his hip-flask.'

'I can tell you that now. It was two-thirds full. Why?'

'Work it out for yourself, Sherlock!'

It took Byron another twenty minutes to reach Lakeside Café. It wasn't busy so he was served quickly and took his food outside, savouring the warm sun on his back. The train he had ridden up on could be heard hooting its approach back to Tanygrisiau; a sound that the hills threw back a few seconds later. He considered getting on it but after a moment's thought decided to stay put. Dylan and his sidekick, Dai Young had plenty enough to get on with and Dylan certainly was quite able to take the initiative. He finished his sausage baguette, brushed off the crumbs and started up the steep road towards the mountains.

The three kids were there again, as they had been last time he wandered up this way. That day had been warm and then they had been in swimming attire splashing around in a pool formed by a small concrete dam higher up in the village.

Byron stepped across the tussocks and boulders strewn around and approached them cautiously. They were all boys, tossing stones into the pool behind the weir. He could hear them swearing good-naturedly at each other. But he would have to tread carefully.

He sat on a rock, poured another coffee and waited. Sure enough the smallest of the three came across. He was clad in expensive hand-me-downs that hung off him.

'Whatcha want Mister?' the boy accosted him. 'You a weirdo?'

'Do I look like a weirdo?' Byron responded mildly.

'Why you watching us, then?'

'Just wondering if you…,' Byron very nearly said, *'come here often,'* which would have sent them running for the nearest Child Protection officer.

'We what?' The child demanded.

'I'm looking for a friend of mine. He likes walking round this place.'

'Must be mad,' the boy replied. 'Dump like this? Nuffin' to do.'

'Well anyway, this friend came past here on Sunday morning, about eleven. Were you here then?'

'Nah. I was visiting my mam. She's in prison.'

'Oh!' Byron felt robbed of speech. The child continued. 'She bit a policeman in his face. Took three of them to arrest her. She don't like policemen.'

'I see.' How long this would have continued, Byron wasn't to discover. The tallest and oldest of the boys came up.

'Shut up lyin' Griff,' he said, grabbing the smaller boy by his arm. He turned to Byron. 'He's always lyin'. Tells teachers at school Dad's in Iraq on a secret mission. People believe him.'

'I'm not lyin,' the smaller boy responded warmly but he was shoved aside.

'You were; I heard you.' He turned to Byron. 'Whatcha want to know?'

Byron repeated his question; at the same time he took out his wallet, removed a banknote and crumpled it in his fist. The older boy's eyes narrowed as he followed the money. 'Might've seen him. Loads of walkers go past here.'

Byron said. 'I'm looking for a man on his own. Not part of a group. He would have come along this road not long after the train had left. About ten past eleven.'

'I saw one man on his own. Had a backpack.'

'Young or old? Describe him.'

The lad had a keen eye. His description of John Coles was fairly clear. He reached out for the note but Byron flicked it away.

'One more question. Which way did he go?'

The lad looked up the road. One way followed a waterfall past huge crumbling walls of slate, mine workings and ramps that led up to the lake. It was just the start of a vast ruined town built to house the labourers and miners when slate was King. The road quickly degraded into a slate-covered rocky path.

The other was a made up road which was barred to cars by a padlocked metal gate. It wound up into the hills, zig-zagging crazily until it reached the top dam of the power station. Byron had walked up this road many times with Marlene. It was at least an hour's hike to the Dam.

'Up that way,' said the youth, pointing to the road.

'How do you know? Did you see him go?'

'Yeah, we were just getting out when he went past. We went home, he was ahead of us. He was a bit funny.'

'Funny? How?'

'Jumpy, kept looking around.'

'He definitely went that way?' Byron asked. The youth nodded and the banknote was his.

'That's one theory down,' Byron thought, looking up at the ribbon of road winding into the high mountains. If it was something to do with mining, he went the wrong way. Most of the shafts and access tunnels were the other side of the mountain.

Also the unprompted observation by the lad that Coles was edgy shed a new light on him. On the CCTV he was calm. Resigned. So perhaps this last walk was the deciding factor. A chance to grapple with the issues that were dogging his life. The comfortable retirement that was dwindling into penury. To someone with a well-paid job, to rely on the basic state pension would be a fall too far. If his wife had been supportive, well most folk could struggle on. But she didn't seem supportive.

Byron glanced at his watch. There was some time to wait before the next train arrived. Why not walk the walk? See afresh what John Coles saw on his last day alive. Breathe the air and try to imagine that after this excursion, he would take his gun and really do what he had planned. Byron surreptitiously patted his stomach – too many biscuits and cake and he needed the exercise.

Last time he came up here with Marlene it took just under an hour to reach the top. That was because Marlene was pushing the pace. This time, sweating and breathless, the front of his legs aching he rounded the last hairpin bend in the road in an hour and twenty.

To Byron's mind, Stwlan Dam resembled the Gates of Mordor in the epic Lord of the Rings movie. It straddled the opening in the mountains; colossal and brutal. It had immense, steeply inclined buttresses that loomed dark and grim with the shadowed recesses between formed into tall arches. At the highest point it was over one hundred feet above the valley floor. A road ran across the top but barriers were in place to deter trespassers. He had passed the footpath leading to Moelwyn Bach off on his left some way back down the road.

In spite of sweating, the sight made Byron shiver. He had been up here in winter and summer, cold days and hot. But the dam always looked impassive, cold and gloomy and frankly gave him the creeps. He turned his back on it and climbed up on the viewpoint that overlooked the road he had just ascended. From this angle it snaked around crazily then dwindled to a thin line in the distance.

Did John Coles bypass this monstrous edifice and head directly up Moelwyn Bach? He might never know, but since he had got this far he might as well walk across the dam. The trouble was, his stomach lurched as he climbed onto the wall to get past the gate barring the road that surmounted the dam wall. On previous occasions he had managed to follow in Marlene's wake, concentrating on her chatter, trying to ignore the physical pain that excessive heights gave him in his guts. Now, with no one for company, the queasiness grew with every step he took onto the titanic wall of Stwlan.

To his right the vast lake flickered in the afternoon sun. The depth gave the water a menacing hue that was dark blue verging on black. To his left the wall guarded a dizzying drop that grew higher the further he went out. He got about a third of the way across when the vertigo hit him for real.

It was as if the thousands of tons of concrete and masonry were slithering around beneath his feet, trying to catapult him into the abyss of water or over the parapet to crash headlong to the rocky floor below. Byron wanted to grasp the wall for support, but the fear intensified as he drew near either edge. Irrational thoughts chased around his head; *'What if it burst now with me on it? After all it won't last for ever!'* His heart racing and more sweat, cold this time, running down his back he forced himself to get his breathing under control. Eventually, by clenching his fists and looking straight ahead of him he managed to walk back the way he had come.

'Well, Byron, lad,' he murmured under his breath as he retraced his steps back down to the foot of the dam wall; *'I'm glad Marlene wasn't here to see that fiasco!'* Above his head the Gates of Mordor remained thankfully closed. Had they decided to open, even just a crack, the lake it held back would have pushed through the opening with a mighty curtain of spray which within a few minutes would have forced the structure wide apart and with a terrifying, sucking roar two million cubic metres of water would begin its rapid and destructive progress down the mountainside.

Several times on the return journey he glanced back up at the dam wall. When he got further down the mountainside, it had slipped out of sight. He stopped and let his gaze return to the wide, rocky valley below him; in spite of all the human activity, it seemed still to be wild and primal. He knew that in its darker moods the mountains could channel colossal amounts of rainwater down their cwms and folds, turning the clear rivers into bellowing, heaving floods that swept over the roads and tore through streets, reminding the residents that they were here on sufferance. Right now, though, it basked in the warm summer sunshine.

John Coles had walked this road and his eyes had seen the same landscape. His ears had heard the fluting whistle of the curlew and the jumble-sale babbling of the sheep. The wailing of the Ffestiniog engine steam sirens would have rolled around these slopes, their rocky faces distorting and lengthening the sound before it faded away. The warm breeze would rustle the leaves on the gnarled moss-laden oak trees and carry the whiff of steam and coal smoke up the slopes to where he stood. He would consult his timetable and decide to walk onwards into Blaenau and meet the last train and when there would decide to sit alone in the last carriage which would be where he would do it. End his life.

Many times in his professional career Byron had encountered suicides. They always depressed him.

Byron called by the Police station on his way back to Gwyneth's B & B. He wanted to check a few things.

'You putting in a bit more overtime, my boy?' he boomed as he saw Dylan hunched over his desk.

'Yes, boss. I got some more stuff for you. Gwen's out there somewhere too; she's been phoning the witnesses all day.'

Dylan had Coles' mobile unlocked and was all for launching into what he had found, but Byron wanted to tidy up a few things before adding fresh data.

'Gwen's witness statements. Anything there?'

'Best from the horse's mouth.' Dylan leaned back and called out; 'Gwen, love, come in yer, will you?' As he relaxed back in his chair, Byron caught his sly grin. He soon found out why.

Gwen Chambers' work was thorough. Exhaustive. Overwhelming. She must have spoken for at least ten minutes to every one of the twenty or so passengers on that train. Every detail had been discovered; where they were staying, how often they came up to the area, whether they had children or grandchildren and even whether they had eating disorders – by the time she had finished with the first class carriage alone even Dylan regretted his mischief.

'Gwen, love, we need to know anything that's unusual, that's all. Did anyone hear anything?'

Gwen looked nonplussed as she scanned her list.

'Yes, indeed. Mrs. Cathy Winters in the third carriage from the back, she was up on holiday with her nephew Richard, although he was down with a bad tummy – she reckons it was that new seafood place although I've eaten there a few times without…'

'What did she say?' Byron didn't mean to snap but it came out anyway. Gwen glared at him then finally said sullenly; 'she remembers hearing a bang,'

Byron sat up. 'When?'

She looked at her notes. 'A few minutes after they stopped in the tunnel. She thought they might have hit a sheep and were shooting it.'

'That's not a bad idea,' Byron reflected out loud. 'If I had my way we'd mount a machine gun on the loco and cut the stupid creatures down. Might suggest it at the next AGM.'

'Is that all, SIR? Only some of us have homes to go to.'

Byron glanced up, taken aback by her tone of voice. He nodded. The door slammed and Hurricane Chambers left the office.

'Did I say something wrong?' he enquired mildly.

Dylan chuckled. 'You and Gwen aren't made for each other. Did you know she was heavily into Animal Rights?'

'No,' Byron lied. 'Anyway, now we can safely say that, however Coles was killed, it was in the tunnel. That accords with the time of death. Any more statements?'

'Nothing of interest. One lady wants to know if she is okay to travel home yet or do we wish her to remain here pending further enquiries.'

'Perhaps we should retain her passport just in case,' was Byron's sardonic reply. 'No, I think anyone on that train who hasn't already gone home can. Okay, that's that. Anything else on medical or financial?'

Dylan shook his head. 'Fit as a flea, but poor as a church mouse.'

'What was Janice's reaction when you told her about the money?'

'Have a guess.'

Byron's first conjecture was correct. Dylan had been favoured with a frozen glare and told something along the lines of;

'Well, I'm really on my own now, aren't I?'

'She was angry, but I suppose she'd been expecting something like this.'

'Ah!' Byron sighed. 'If only folk would talk to each other. What else?'

Dylan held up the phone. 'This, Sir.'

'Well, before you hit me with that, have you eaten? 'Cause I'm ravenous and the Chinese takeaway here is second to none. What say we order, I collect and pick up a couple of beers and we make a working dinner of it?'

Dylan had no objections.

'Gwen'll kick up a stink tomorrow unless we get rid of this smell.' Dylan threw open the window. The evening air was pleasantly cool and the noise of traffic subdued. Unable to contain their hunger they had eaten most of the meal without discussing anything further.

'This is a two beer problem,' Byron announced at last, reaching for the rest of the four-pack on the floor beside his chair and tossing one to Dylan. 'So, what's the phone got to tell us?'

Dylan placed it on the desk in front of Byron.

'To be honest, not a lot.'

If John Edward Coles was up to anything underhand, he was being remarkably coy about it. The smartphone was not an expensive model, neither was it a rip-off cheap copy. It was middle of the road useful without being flashy. Predictably the opening wallpaper was one of a number that came with the phone and only a few icons were downloaded. Train travel, interactive maps, 'where's my plane,' weather and a few more.

They viewed his messages. With a heavy heart Byron confirmed what he had suspected – a dry, loveless marriage. Janice would text questions like;

'Are you planning to come back anytime?'

After a few days the slightly mocking reply;

'Don't wait up.'

Occasionally interspersed with more helpful bouts of communication such as when the car was giving trouble, John would make enquiries and get it seen to. But in the main, the impression given of their marriage by the Black Widow, as Dylan was apt to call her, was continued in their private correspondence.

'Life and soul of the party, both of them,' Byron muttered.

'But probably not at the same party,' was Dylan's pithy reply.

There were phone calls from various places – some in Eastern Europe which Dylan was tasked with following up and two or three dozen contacts. But no 'bit on the side,' no flirtatious messages, salacious whispers or anything that suggested any romantic interest.

'He was seventy!' Byron protested. 'If you're still hot stuff by then, I'll warn my granddaughters about you.'

Almost the last place they looked was the only nugget of interest. Coles kept a list of electronic notes on his mobile. Passwords, reminders, jobs to be done and general notes to himself.

Halfway down the list was a file with no title which had two entries. The first was a string of fourteen letters. The second the message;

'1000 to bring it down at 10'

'Well what do you make of that?' Dylan wondered. He cleared the detritus from the Chinese and in so doing discovered that they had a second bag of prawn crackers. 'D'you want any of these?'

Byron shook his head. *'1000 to bring it down at 10.'* Bring what down and why such a specific time?

'Drugs shipment?' his companion asked.

'If it is, for a thousand quid he's scarcely in the big league. What car did he drive when he could?'

'Second hand Volkswagen. Hardly a babe magnet.'

They tussled with the two cryptic messages for half an hour, but as Byron pointed out, they were his notes, *aide memoires* so to speak, and certainly only of use to himself.

'Let's leave it,' said Byron eventually. 'Sleep on it. What else do we have?'

'Toxicology report and time of death.'

'And..?'

'He died in the early evening. Apart from a cheese baguette consumed at lunchtime, nothing in his stomach or bloodstream to cause drowsiness. I asked, you see, when you said about him being shot with his own gun. Struck me that if he had been drugged, that would be possible.'

'Good man. Another door closes, then.'

'Did you find out where he went on Sunday?' Dylan asked when the last of the prawn crackers were finished. Byron related his conversation with the kids at the pool.

'I know that family,' he said. 'Youngest kid is a congenital liar. Mind you, mam's not much better. So did they help?'

The oldest did, Byron explained, relating how he took the path up to the dam. He omitted to mention that he comprehensively freaked out at the top. Dylan was impressed all the same.

'You're no couch potato, are you, Sir? Like your walking then?'

Byron stretched himself and told him of Marlene's influence on him. Long, vigorous hikes in all weathers. Cycle rides, even running. She dragged him out. Until recently that was.

'Not that it has any effect,' he said sadly, looking at his round belly. 'But here's a little puzzle for you.'

Dylan took a gulp of beer. 'Fire away, Sir.'

'Those kids saw Coles about eleven o' clock. It took me well over an hour to get to the dam which was the road he headed up. I've seen him striding off a couple of times and I tell you he's fast. He could have been up there by midday...'

'Presuming he went there...'

'Yes, I'm coming to that. Okay, allowing for the time he had there are only a few possibilities. He could have branched off the road to the footpath that leads over Moelwyn Mawr and Moelwyn Bach. Have you been up there?'

Dylan shook his head. 'Not my kind of thing, Sir.'

'Well, if you go that way, it's a linear walk down to the Croesor Road which brings you back at Tan y Bwlch, you know, the station in the woods.'

What was a linear walk, his colleague wanted to know. Byron explained that to any hard-bitten walker, it was usually preferable to follow a linear course that took you to a particular destination or a circular route back to where you started. The next sighting of Coles was in Blaenau at six o' clock. Which was the opposite direction to the Mawr and Bach mountains.

'So maybe he climbed the mountains then came back the same way.'

Byron nodded. 'I agree. But it doesn't feel right. If you walk you don't often retrace your steps, especially if you have time on your hands. If I had my maps I could work out a possible circuit that would bring him over Crag Nyth and down to Blaenau Ffestiniog, but...'

'But what, Sir?'

'That doesn't feel right either. If he'd wanted to go there, he would have gone up the other track to the slate mines.'

'Maybe he went over the top?'

Byron laughed. 'Spoken like a lowlander! Those are serious inclines. You would need ropes and climbing gear, and I'm certain as I can be he carried nothing like that.'

'So what are you saying he did?'

Byron shrugged. 'It looks to me like he walked up somewhere, stayed around for two or three hours then came back down the same way. Which is strange.' The moment he said it, Byron was conscious he was violating his own rules. People were unpredictable. Where was it decreed that Coles had to do a planned, circular or linear walk? Perhaps melancholy overcame him and he just settled down on a hillside or mountain top and watched the last afternoon of his life slip by.

'Maybe he changed his plans when he saw the weather was turning. Let's move on,' Byron said.

David Young's enquiries weren't very productive either. His report showed that the Travelodge staff were security conscious and able to supply CCTV footage and door swipe logs to show that Coles' room had not been entered since he left Sunday morning. He specifically asked that cleaners and bed makers not go in there. Part of the reason they were anxious to cooperate, David said, was that they wanted the room cleared of his effects.

'We'll go tomorrow, first thing,' Byron promised.

That just left the other question that Byron had pondered about. If this was an organised killing, which was looking increasingly unlikely as time went on; then how could it have been arranged so effectively? So many things needed to be right. Notwithstanding the difficulty of obtaining Coles' weapon and shooting him with it, how could the assassins be confident he was alone in that carriage and would remain so? Someone must have been hovering around the station when he boarded the train, been able to report to the others that their target was not only isolated but out of earshot of the rest of the train. Had Coles decided to travel first class, then all the sheep in Snowdonia would not suffice as a distraction. He would have been in full view and therefore protected.

'Got to be home just yet?' He asked Dylan.

'The wood burner won't run away,' he replied.

'Good, let's check the CCTV at Blaenau again. We need the loiterer if there is one.'

An hour later, eyes aching from straining to view the fuzzy images they both agreed to call it a day. There were people who seemed to hang around the station, but they were doing what Byron recognised from years of experience – being random human beings. They lingered, dived into the shop, made mobile phone calls, took calls and one couple even seemed to be having a domestic right in front of the camera.

'Let's face it,' Dylan sighed, 'if they're professionals, they'd keep out of view of the cameras anyway so this is probably a waste of time.' He chewed his fingers and cracked his knuckles.

'Coles' hotel room, first thing tomorrow, then,' Byron snapped the laptop lid down and yawned. 'Out of interest, have you enjoyed the train rides?'

The gleam in his companion's eyes and his sudden animation assured him that Dylan had discovered that playing trains was not something you grew out of. He had a question.

'What's this gravity thing they're doing tomorrow, Sir? It sounds fun. I was watching a vid of it earlier.'

The Gravity Train was an activity put on by volunteers and staff of the railway that reached back to the very earliest days of the line. Before there were locomotives, before there were passenger services when the track was a just railed incline that descended gently for its entire length from the slate mines at Blaenau Ffestiniog down to the harbour at Porthmadog. Then, slate would be loaded into open wagons and hitched together with a brake at the rear. The heavy wagons would be allowed to roll under gravity down the track. Obviously they would gain speed and with the sharp curves of the track would soon derail, so a 'brakesman' rode the wagons, holding the speed down by means of a lever that applied wooden blocks to the wheels. Once down, the wagons were unloaded and hauled back up by ponies.

It was a dangerous operation. If the brakes got too hot they would catch fire so they were doused with water regularly. If the system failed, the unfortunate brakesman was riding a runaway weighing several tons. His only hope was to leap off if he could and let the whole thing find its own way down the mountain. These were pioneering times when life was cheap and nothing was done for fun, but the modern process of recreating the original gravity slate trains was a great deal safer.

Tomorrow, a selected few would ride the gravity trains down from the highest point of the track, just behind the Power Station, coasting sedately down the incline as far as Rhiw Goch where the track spanned a high viaduct. This section of the railway was almost devoid of line side houses and deemed safe to use as practice for the function.

'You can come along if you want,' Byron told his colleague. 'I'm allowed a guest.'

CHAPTER 7

'WHATCHA GOT FOR ME SHERLOCK?'

Byron yawned. The sea air did make him drowsy. Marlene, on the other hand, had been nowhere and was in need of an outlet.

'It's looking more self-inflicted the more we go on.'

'I see. What great weight of evidence has brought you to this conclusion?'

Byron ran past her the case details. He was conscious he was loading his account towards suicide.

'So when this kid by the pool said Coles was jumpy, that didn't make you think?' She said, her voice sharp.

'Of course it did, but it fitted with the pattern...'

'Thought you didn't believe in patterns. People are random, that's your line!'

'No, I don't set scientific store by believing that people do things unfailingly when prompted by external circumstances.' Byron could feel his patience ebbing. 'It leads you in the wrong direction.'

'Well I think you're heading in the same, wrong direction. Explain to me why he was edgy when the kids saw him, but calm when you checked his ticket.'

'John Coles was suicidal, love. Plain and simple. He's having his last walk up places he loves. Of course he's jittery. He spends two or three hours up there and comes back the same way. But by the time he returns he's ready to go through with it.'

'Shall I tell you my take on it?'

'You're going to anyway.' The moment the words were past his lips Byron regretted it.

'Listen oh great detective, I think you're making the biggest mistake of your career. You're missing something, I don't know what, but you're missing it all the same.'

'If I run with this claim that it was a planned killing for reason or reasons unknown, and they ship in a whole investigative team from the riot zones, how do you think that'll make me look? A hysterical idiot! It would be a fitting finale to a fading career. No, Marlene, I'd rather go out with a whimper than a bang that fizzled out.'

'You're not looking at all the data!' She was almost yelling down the phone.

'Okay, tell me what I've overlooked, then!'

'He bought a season ticket for the railway. They're not expensive, I know, but when money is short and you're not planning on seeing the summer out, why would you spend that money? Oh, I know some people top themselves on the spur of the moment, but you know Coles isn't that type. If he was contemplating suicide, he'd hardly plan another year of train rides at the same time. Same for those spirits in his flask… What was it?'

'Brandy,' Byron said, aware he was sounding sulky.

'Okay, not all people are alike, but taking your own life is a big step, yeah? You need lots of Dutch courage. So why didn't he drink more of it? At least half, two thirds would be better. Conclusion; he wasn't intending to take his life. Conclusion two; someone took it for him.'

It was verging on a row and Byron didn't want to go there. He pacified, grovelled and finally apologised whilst firmly maintaining that he still had to go with the available evidence and that Superintendent Gwillim Ward was breathing down Dylan's neck for an outcome.

'You can't win every time, love.'

'What were those letters and the strange sentence again?' She demanded.

Byron told her the letters, checking each off as she wrote them down. The sentence had been floating around his head all evening and came readily to his lips;

'1000 to bring it down at 10'

'Leave it with me,' she said and rang off.

Byron and Dylan could sense the relief on the duty manager's face as he led them to the upstairs room recently vacated by John Coles. The room had been checked for fingerprints but apart from the traces of dust was exactly as he had left it. With rubber gloves on they lifted items of his clothing, ran their fingers through pockets and patted jacket linings. They examined his washing and shaving materials, sniffing and scrutinising each item minutely. Fingerprints had ruled out the window as a means of entry – anyway it had an anti-theft latch that allowed it to open only a few centimetres. After an hour they looked at each other.

'If this were a movie, boss, one of us would discover the rare cockroach or unusual tie-pin that would lead us to the mafia or whoever did this,' was Dylan's best attempt at humour. Byron grunted by way of reply. Finally he concluded,

'Nothing to see here. Let's give them the room back. Pack this stuff up and we'll have another look when we get back to the station. Oh, are they for us?'

The duty manager had appeared with a tray of coffee and Danish pastries. Clearly an incentive to help them on their way. He was delighted when Byron informed him that they were packing up.

'Will you take these in the breakfast room, then?' he beamed.

Ten minutes later they were seated and enjoying their early elevenses. Coles' stuff was in two bin bags in the back of the car and ready for Dai Young to check over.

'So where are we at?' Dylan wanted to know.

Byron sighed. 'Honestly? I don't know. We have motive and means for suicide.'

'Rubbish marriage, dwindling assets. Own weapon to hand,' Dylan supplied.

'Good. Keep talking, it helps me. Now tell me the objections.'

'Not the best of prints and less powder residue than would be expected on his right hand.'

'Which could be explained by…'

'Dry skin and some types of gun don't blow back as much.'

'Any other objections to suicide?'

'He seemed too calm.'

'Which the lad I spoke to answered by his unsolicited comment that he seemed agitated earlier. No, I need something more specific.'

Dylan mused. 'Doesn't seem the type?'

'No, that doesn't hold. There are no hard and fast rules to say who would do it. No I've got a couple of other minor things.'

Feeling rather guilty he related Marlene's theories about the season ticket and the amount of brandy left in the flask. He felt even more awkward when Dylan was impressed with the conjecture.

'Very good! That's almost like in the films, Sir. I mean it doesn't prove anything for certain but it does help you see the possibility of another explanation.'

'Talking of which, we need to do the pro's and con's for the other theory. So off you go.'

'Coles falls foul of a gang who drive sheep onto the line to create a distraction during which they shoot him in the head with his own gun. That would answer the low powder residue on the victim's hand and also why he was relaxed. He wasn't expecting trouble then.'

'And the case against this?'

'It would need some slick organisation, Sir. Really clever to pull it off if you ask me. They'd have to know for sure he was alone, then they'd have to grab his gun – how would they know where it was or even if he had it with him? They only get one chance and there's the risk he might get to it first. We've ruled out doping him, so how did they pull it off? Is that about it?'

'It's enough for me.' Byron felt a sinking feeling that another row with Marlene was imminent. 'Our cryptic message is probably irrelevant. We have no criminal record and apart from those phone records...'

'Which are mostly Eastern European mining suppliers. I checked online last night.'

'Good. Are they kosher?'

'Not easy to tell, Sir. I have a few contacts in the Midlands who know more about this sort of thing. If they come back to me I'll let you know.'

Byron warmed his hands around the coffee mug and dabbed his finger in the crumbs of his Danish to wipe them up.

'Did you find out what a mining engineer does?' He asked at length.

'Next thing on the list, Sir.'

When they arrived back at the station, Dai Young was already hard at work. The reason soon became clear.

'Super's here,' he nodded towards the staff rest area. 'Think he's looking for a result.'

'There's only one result he wants to hear,' thought Byron, heading for the tea room with its scruffy, broken down armchairs and coffee stained table.

Gwillim Ward tried to give the impression of relaxed *bonhomie*, but it was obvious he was under strain. A few pleasantries were exchanged then he said;

'I take it we're on course for wrapping this case up?'

'Wish Marlene was here,' thought Byron, acutely aware that Gwillim was in a difficult position. The unrest caused by the hydro-electric proposals was showing no signs of abating and he frankly had neither the resources nor time to spare a single member of staff. In an ideal world, he would probably have been just as curious as Byron to nail the discrepancies in the events leading to the death of John Coles. But not now.

'Let me just run what we know past you,' Byron suggested.

Ten minutes later, during which Gwillim politely listened, Byron felt that things had reached an outcome. He was about to say this when Gwillim cleared his throat in the manner of someone who has a difficult speech to make.

'Byron,' he said. 'I can see why you feel there's more to this than meets the eye. I'm really obliged to you, you've done a sterling job…'

'You'd better tell Dylan Woods that,' said Byron, jerking his thumb over his shoulder. 'He's done the real legwork. I tell you he has the makings of an outstanding detective.'

'Yes, yes. But I feel uncomfortable taking up more of your time. You were on holiday, dammit. It's not my call, but I don't want you to feel you have to continue.'

He stumbled on, phrasing his request in diplomatic language. The case was dead, in his opinion and he needed his officers back on more pressing issues.

'There's one or two things I need to tie up, then I'll be off,' Byron reassured him. His mobile rang. 'Will you excuse me. I need to take this.'

Gwillim shook his hand in a perfunctory way and slipped out to talk with Dylan.

'Jason,' – it was his stand-in back at the railway. 'How's things?'

Jason was harassed. Things were going wrong – the chip shop that supplied the Fish and Chip Special train had had a fire, and were unable to open for the rest of the week. Some kids had climbed onto the shed roof at Minffordd and damaged the fragile boards. Another lorry had broken down on the Britannia Terrace, blocking the Welsh Highland line for the second time in as many weeks, proving that lightning does strike twice in the same place. Byron talked through the problems, offering advice where needed and reassuring him that he was coping splendidly.

'I should be back before long,' he said quietly. 'Things are winding up here.'

'Just as well, we're another man… sorry woman, down.'

When Byron heard that Marta had not shown up for work that morning, his initial reaction was one of surprise. Marta was definitely a showcase of reliability and hard work. He communicated this to Jason, but after a moment's thought pointed out;

'Well, she's due a break. I've told her, you've told her often enough. What with this all happening perhaps she's taken the hint at last.'

'That's fine,' came back the grumbled reply. 'But let me know at least. She met this bloke last night, went off with him and now I have to shuffle folk around.'

'Who did she meet? One of the volunteers?'

'Hang on;' Byron heard Jason calling round the office for more information. He came back; 'no one we know. Sue, here says they seemed to know each other well enough though.'

'Could this be the two-faced, Huw?' Byron wondered. 'Look, Jason, you're doing just fine. Hang on in there and I'll be along just as soon as I can.'

When he returned to the office, Dylan was tidying his desk. He glanced up.

'Marching orders, Sir,' he said, trying to look happy. 'John Coles and his gang of assassins are all yours, more's the pity. I must say, though, I've really enjoyed working with you on this. Wish it could have been longer. Perhaps you should come yer on holiday again and I'll keep some work by for you - as long as we can use your office, that is.'

'Where's Gwillim?'

'The Super had to go. What are your plans, Sir?'

Byron shrugged. The case had been fun whilst it lasted, but now it had been not terminated but dismissed as of little importance. He no longer felt any interest in why Coles had been found dead in the last carriage of the last train of Saturday night. He would go back to his railway duties and leave the dead to bury their dead.

'1000 to bring it down at 10,' he muttered absently.

'What's that?' asked Dylan.

'Oh, nothing now.' Byron logged into his desktop and began thinking about the report.

Dylan was about to leave when he said; 'we still good for tonight?'

'Tonight?'

'Those gravity trains. Is it okay for me to come along? Only the missus is shopping in Chester with her buddies and set to make an evening of it. Got nothing much to do apart from that wood burner.'

'Oh yes, of course. We're running from the summit to Rhiw Goch. We can park up at Penrhyn. I'll take you there. Six o' clock.'

'Sure thing!' Dylan left quickly to avoid being accosted by Gwen on the way out.

No matter how many tweaks he made to the report, Byron felt it was a weak, haphazard summary. He was supposed to guide the North Wales Police to a clear decision as to whether to prosecute a further investigation or drop the whole thing. His inclination was to prune his observations so that the conclusion; 'suicide' would just be a natural outcome. But honesty dictated he include the difficult features that had dogged this investigation.

He caught himself biting his nails. Dylan's habit was rubbing off on him. Two or three discrepancies – not major but nevertheless there, like grit in his shoe, niggling at him with each step he took. They went round and round his mind, distracting him from the task in hand.

'He was too relaxed.'

'He only drank a little of his brandy...'

'He renewed his season ticket.'

He fought them back; *'people don't conform. Not all suicides are sweating blood at the finish. They don't have to drink themselves witless to go through with it...'*

But the last discrepancy niggled him the most. A season ticket – the guarantee of a year's free travel on the railway. If you were not railway mad you would be unlikely to buy one. If you did then why would you cut your life short when you had nearly a year left to go? It wasn't as if Coles' crisis had come upon him suddenly, he had bought the ticket in full knowledge that money was running short and it made sound financial sense. So why not use it?

Somehow he got to the end of his report, read it, re-read it then finally and with a glum sigh hit 'SEND.'

It was mid-afternoon by the time Byron had finished filling in his expenses form. He said a hasty goodbye to Gwen who barely cracked a smile in return and wandered out into the High Street to get some lunch. David Young had gone to the chemists to get something for a headache so not a civil send off there either. He felt at a loose end; the sense of anti-climax that usually dogged him at the end of a case. The antidote was work; to throw himself back into the railway and give the long-suffering Jason a break. Trouble was that the day was far gone in that respect. To turn up now would intrude on others' arrangements and make him feel in the way. Besides which there was another phone call to make. He commandeered a bench overlooking the crazy golf and dialled her.

'You bottled it then?' Marlene was nothing, if not direct.

'If you want to put it that way.'

'Well don't say I didn't warn you!'

'Warn me?' Byron replied irritably. 'What do you suppose is going to happen now I've directed Gwillim to record it as suicide? Will Coles climb out of the fridge and denounce me?'

'Byron, If I haven't made it clear then listen to what I think – this was planned, cold-blooded execution. Expertly done by people who covered their tracks well...'

'So well that nothing remained...' Byron muttered. She ignored him.

'They were playing a dangerous game, high stakes; think of a cliché and it applies to this one. They needed Coles dead but in a way that nothing could point to foul play. Why? Obviously Coles had information on something they were intending to do. Maybe a huge drugs operation, I don't know.'

'Hence a thousand to bring it down at ten;' in spite of himself, Byron felt interest stirring afresh. She continued;

'Whatever that means. But they didn't just do him in on top of a lonely mountain, did they? He thought they might try to, hence he was nervous and most likely carried the gun with him. This suggests that he knew how to use it. To get near enough to shoot him would be near enough to get shot back. So he carries on to Blaenau. By the time you check his ticket, he thinks the danger is passed and has a nip or two to celebrate. You with me so far?'

'So why make it look like suicide?'

'To buy time. I'm going to put my head above the parapet and make a bet.'

'Usual stakes?' When Byron and Marlene took a wager, the loser took the other to a restaurant of choice. If Marlene was paying she could relax, Byron's choice of cuisine usually ended at the local pub by the river. But Marlene had more expensive tastes. She agreed.

'You've got Coles' phone, yes? But nothing much on there. All very clean and above board and too good to be true. I bet there's another one. One he would use to call a contact who would check him in to make sure nothing had befallen him, like a stray bullet for example.'

'Wait a moment,' Byron protested. 'Another phone? How are we going to find that? And if we don't you can't say you win the bet.'

'Okay, so I bet that if you check Janice Coles' own mobile or landline numbers, you'll find that every day he called her.'

It took a moment for the implication to sink in. 'You're saying she's involved in whatever he was up to?' Byron felt the urgent need to sit down, then realised he already was.

'Right up to her starched, buttoned-up collar.'

'You'd better have a good explanation,' he sighed.

Something was being planned, she surmised, trying to make it sound as though everything was clear in her mind. Something that depended on a time schedule. Coles' involvement was as a purchaser, a supplier of materials, whatever they might be. Janice was poised to blow the whistle should things backfire. If he failed to check in with his nightly phone call, she was to cry foul play and start the search for his body.

'But we were investigating a suicide,' Byron breathed.

'Exactly! Not that Janice believed it for a moment, but she could hardly say anything about it could she? To do so would set the keen, relentless searchers for truth onto her as well.'

Byron ignored the subtle jibe.

'The simulated suicide gives whoever did this time. Breathing space to finish whatever they needed to do. Whatever Coles' part was in this, and I'm guessing he was in way over his head, he had to be cleared out of the way with no suspicion on any outside agency. And you, dear husband, bought the lie.'

'Or, alternatively, your dear husband saw the simple, plain truth and concluded accordingly.'

'Check Janice's phones. Might not even be a spoken call, just a few rings to say, 'I'm alive.' I'm going to book that new bistro down by the reservoir.'

'You sound very sure of yourself.'

'I am. I feel it in my crumbling bones, something very unpleasant is brewing up your way. So get digging again Sherlock.'

'Porthmadog Police, DC Dylan Woods here. How can I help?'

It sounded very professional. Byron grinned. 'I was expecting Dai Young. Gwillim changed his mind about deploying you?'

'Byron!' Dylan sounded pleased. 'No, it's off to the trenches tomorrow. But I called in some lieu time so I would be around for this evening.'

'You busy?'

'Nothing that won't wait. Why?'

Byron could hear the delight in Woods' voice as he explained what he wanted done.

'Won't take long. I'll have the call log by the time you're here.'

He was true to his word. Byron scanned the list of calls to Janice Coles' residence.

'Interview room, Sir?' asked Dylan gleefully.

'I don't see why not.'

An hour later, they watched a stony-faced Janice Coles as she sat bolt upright in the room behind the one-way glass. 'Who's going to interrogate whom,' wondered Byron as they entered.

'Mrs Coles…' Byron began.

'Will this take long? I was preparing to go home now you have released my husband's remains.'

'I hope not.' Byron took one of the two chairs facing her on the other side of the table. Dylan swung his round and hunched over the back.

'We just need to ask a few more questions, Mrs Coles. Can I call you Janice?'

'If you must.'

'Good. Now, Janice, can you recall the last time your husband contacted you?'

Her eyes narrowed. 'As you still have his phone you should be able to tell me that.'

'Okay,' Byron soothed, 'Dylan, can you tell me the date of the last communication from John Coles to his wife, please?'

Dylan made a show of tapping on the keys of the smartphone they had taken from the deceased. 'Thursday twenty-second, eleven am, text message reads; *'Staying a few more days.'* He did not receive a reply.'

'Does that correspond with your recollections, Janice?'

She shrugged. Byron persisted;

'So no other communications from your late husband in the days leading up to his death?'

'Nothing I can recall.'

'Dylan, can you read out a few of the entries in the log of Janice's own mobile and landline phones, please.'

Woods gleefully did so, rattling off a string of short log entries. Mostly about five or six in the evening, sometimes just a few rings then nothing. Now and then for a few seconds the call was answered before the line was quickly closed. Each entry originated from an identical number which Dylan read out remorselessly. The last was the Saturday just gone a few minutes before he was dead. At this Janice had had enough.

'Stop!' she hissed. 'What is the meaning of this?' She had flushed slightly.

'You tell us,' Byron suggested mildly. 'Every day a mobile number calls you either at the home number or your mobile. A few rings, then nothing. Is it a signal?'

If she was rattled she did not for a moment show it. 'My husband has… had two phones,' she said, not taking her eyes off Byron who returned her stare. 'He originally had an old flip-top phone which he kept on him all the time. The battery lasted for weeks, or so he told me. I bought him the new phone as a present because he needed to know times of trains and public transport since he… well,'

'Lost his licence,' Dylan supplied.

'He went off alone on long walks through areas not frequented by tourists,' she went on. 'Not that I minded, he did as he pleased. But not being young any more I insisted he signal me at the end of each walk so that I knew he had come to no harm. His new phone needed nightly charging but he was apt to forget, so he would use the old phone to send the signal. Does that answer your question?'

'You could have told us this earlier,' Byron murmured.

'Is it relevant?'

'That's for us to decide. Do you know the whereabouts of this phone?'

She shook her head. 'I thought you had all my husband's effects.'

'There was only one phone,' Dylan supplied.

'So the missing one, by now, is probably at the bottom of the deepest lake in Snowdonia,' Byron thought despondently. He leaned across the table, placing his fingertips together in an arch.

'Mrs Coles, do you have any reason to believe your husband's death was anything other than suicide?'

'Why are you asking me this? I was of the impression that we paid our taxes for your officers to find out that.'

'Will you excuse us, madam?' Byron hauled Dylan out of the room.

'She's good,' he said, half in admiration, half in annoyance looking at her through the mirrored window.

'You going to charge her, Sir?'

'With what? Withholding information vital to an investigation? Wasting police time? That would waste some more of our time. I'd like to drop 'accessory to a murder' on her and see if that would make her flinch. Anyway…' he shrugged, 'you got any questions for her?'

Dylan hadn't but as they returned to the room, Byron began to feel reckless;

'Janice,' he began. The implacable stare came to rest on him. 'Are you aware that your husband had another bank account besides the ones we have shown you?'

The effect was even more startling than when she had been confronted with the gun. She half-stood, clutching the table for support.

'Where is it? How much is in there?'

'I'm sorry, I'm not at liberty to tell you right now, but thank you for confirming that for me. Dylan, would you show Mrs Coles out? And Janice…?'

For the first time since they had met, Janice Coles looked seriously rattled. She meekly agreed to remain in the vicinity for a few more days until their enquiries were complete. As she left there was less iron in her backbone than when she arrived.

'You bluffed about that bank account, didn't you?' Dylan sounded gleeful.

'It was a shot in the dark,' Byron admitted. 'But now, if you've got some spare time, you need to dig around.'

'Why didn't you just question her? She could be lying.'

'And have her say to me; 'Sir, I am a mathematics teacher, not an accountant,' or something like that?' Byron shuddered. 'No, somehow or other we can find that account and see if John Coles was as poor as he looks.'

'I'm on it, Sir!' Dylan sat down at his desk, logged into his computer and began tapping at the keys.

'It would be easy if we had that other phone, though.' Byron excused himself and left the room. 'Got to go, I have a call to make.'

'I've booked Reservoir Bistro,' she crowed. 'It's very expensive!'

'Smugness doesn't suit you,' he grumbled. 'So what are you thinking?'

'Ah! At last my dear husband is coming to heel. You could be a top detective yet.'

'Seriously, you think something nasty's on the cards? I need to know.'

'I do.' The triumphant note vanished from her voice. She sounded subdued. 'Byron, love, I'm worried. For you, I mean.'

'Why?'

'Whatever this is; drugs, people trafficking, terrorism – you're the only one facing them. It shouldn't be like this. You should have armed backup, top-level surveillance, whatever it takes.'

'Thereby hangs our problem, there's no slack.'

'Yes there is. There always is. Hit the alarm bell, get people down there. Tell them that some major operation is going on. They'll believe you. Don't go it alone just because you're afraid you might look a fool.'

'What is going on? They'd need to know before they commit resources.'

'Can you get to your emails?'

'No problem. I'll just get the laptop. Why?'

'I'll send you something. Stay on the line.'

The message was not long. It was scanned from monthly journal that catered for the world of mining. The magazine was still being produced and no doubt avidly read by everyone from quarry managers to mining executives. Pictures of huge trucks with tyres the size of small cars priced in dollars. Reports on projects around the world with eye-watering price tags. Comment and advice on dealing with unusual folds in strata or legal staffing level requirements. It had a multitude of advertisements for machinery, dust and fume extraction equipment, personal safety gear, roof supports, drainage and pumping solutions – everything that those who ventured deep into the bowels of the earth would need to ensure safe working conditions whilst still turning a handsome profit. The issue on the screen before him was dated from eight years ago.

'Page seventeen, retirement notices for the UK,' Marlene directed him.

There he was, John Edward Coles and a string of professional qualifications. Brief résumé of his early and mid-career and a few glowing tributes from staff who knew him. Pretty much the same sort of thing Byron would hope for himself just as soon as he could swing a decent deal from his force.

'Seen his speciality?' Marlene asked.

There it was, a tribute to a man who was trusted implicitly by his colleagues because he had to be. Experience and expertise combined with a meticulous level-headed professionalism when it was needed most.

'He was an explosives expert,' Byron breathed. 'Oh…'

'You need backup, love. Please!'

Byron sat in the lumpy collapsed armchair in the rest room and digested this new piece of information.

Dylan was enthusiastic about this latest development. His theories became more and more outlandish;

'Illegal mining, boss. You know the sort of thing…'

Byron didn't and it became clear Dylan didn't either. Nor did he know how mining operatives went about obtaining explosives. The revelation, if it was a revelation, that John Coles dealt with the procurement and deployment of high grade mining explosives and detonators felt important – but could be entirely benign. After all, mines needed explosives, presumably they bought them from legitimate sources, carefully controlled and used them in accordance with established procedure. Just because he was part of this chain didn't make Coles a terrorist as Dylan was now conjecturing. But it did add a worrying aspect to the case.

To appease Marlene, Byron tried to ring Superintendent Gwillim Ward, but just got voicemail. He left a message:

'Byron Unsworth here. I sent you a report. Don't disregard it, but there has been a little bit more material I'm following up. Ring me when you pick this up.'

'Time to play trains, Sir.' Dylan looked ecstatic.

CHAPTER 8

'PHIL BRAITHEWAITE'S running this operation,' Byron said as he eased the car into the small space alongside the station building at Penrhyn. 'Ex-marine engineering and takes no prisoners. So do as you're told.'

'Yes, SIRR!' Dylan, in the front seat, snapped to attention with a scrappy salute.

'Save that for Phil, if you dare. Come on, this way.'

The train was waiting at the station – the locomotive 'Lyd' steaming away at the front coupled to a string of open wagons that disappeared round the corner. Sue, the harbour station secretary saw them arrive and bustled up with a clipboard.

'Marta worked out the list. You're meant to be riding with her, but she's not here.'

'I know. I think she's having a reconciliation. At least I hope so. But Dylan here will stand in for her, even if his legs are nowhere near as shapely.'

Predictably, Sue missed the witticism. 'Is he new to this? Has he had induction?'

'Yes and no.' Byron replied. 'Phil can run through the basics with him, then if he still wants to ride he can. He's my guest, you see.'

'Okay,' Sue looked askance at her list. 'I'll put him with you, is that okay? You were allocated the last four wagons.'

Byron had no objections, Dylan was propelled in the direction of Phil Braithewaite who was a small, wiry, thin-faced man who wasted no time in going through the formalities and issuing him a hard hat and high-vis jacket. Then, as a larger group of volunteers and staff assembled, he corralled them together under the station awning and addressed them.

'Okay, so this is a practice run for the Victorian Weekend.' His voice was surprisingly soft, but it was well-known that he kept the full volume back for anyone who saw fit to talk over him. 'We have twenty wagons here with us, mostly loaded to typical running weight. We'll be taking four wagons down at a time with two brakesmen. On the day we'll be running one complete train all the way to the harbour, but so's that everyone gets a go, this evening we'll be running separates. You've been assigned one experienced operator and one novice to each set of wagons.'

He glanced at some notes he was holding, deciding what to include and what to leave out.

'You'll each be given a walkie-talkie. You leave when I tell you to and not a moment sooner. Top speed is fifteen miles per hour...'

'Question,' someone called, then added tentatively, 'Sir.'

'Fire away.'

'How will we know when we're at fifteen miles an hour?'

Phil Braithewaite chewed his lip, then said;

'You'll know all right. As you know, the track is narrow with high walls for some of the way and sharp twists and turns. Furthermore, these carriages are entirely unsprung. It will be like a rollercoaster ride. Every jolt and rattle will be transmitted to you so that by the time you reach the end your fillings will be falling out and your brains coming loose. I assure you you will not wish to exceed the speed limit, but if you feel the urge to try...' he produced a stop watch. 'I have timed the journey at thirty minutes. From the moment I say go I will set this watch running. Should you arrive before the time, then you will be struck off the list for the Victorian weekend. That, ladies and gentlemen is a promise.'

He went on to explain that the train, complete with operators would ascend shortly but then wait at Tan y Bwlch for the last down train to pass, then they would go up to the summit. Four carriages would be uncoupled at a time and allowed to descend when Phil gave the signal.

'All clear, ladies and gentlemen?' Receiving only a muted murmur he threw his head back and bawled;

'IS THIS CLEAR?'

'Yes, Sir!' the group cried as one.

'He's a big softy, really,' Byron whispered to Dylan as they climbed aboard the first four wagons behind the locomotive. 'Known him since we were at school together.'

As Phil had warned, the ride was extremely rough. Every jolt from the rail joints transmitted itself remorselessly through the metalwork and into their bones. The journey up was slow as Lyd strained against the weight of the wagons. Many were full with slate, neatly stacked upright like magazines on a shelf whereas others had large tanks of water to make up mass. They were glad when the train halted at Tan y Bwlch to take on water and await the down train from Blaenau.

'I feel like I've done ten rounds with Terry Donovan,' Dylan groaned as they stretched themselves.

'Terry who?'

'Oh, lad from town; you don't want to meet him after he's had a few. Ah! Is this the down train?'

David Lloyd George coasted round the corner and shuddered to a stop in the station. As on Sunday night, a few folk disembarked and headed for their cars, the rest watched with frank curiosity as the Gravity Train and its riders began to chug up towards the summit.

'If it's like this going up;' Dylan squatted on his haunches in the back of the wagon trying to cushion himself against the hammer-blows from the track, 'what's going down going to be like?'

'That's what you're about to find out,' Byron grinned wickedly although from experience he knew that the higher speeds of the descent tended to reduce the harshness of the jolting. 'Look on the bright side, though,' he pointed to the engine ahead, belching out steam and smoke as it fought the incline. 'At least we're not getting much of that. About halfway back is where the soot drops.'

Way back along the creaking wagons, their wheel flanges singing against the rails as they snaked up the tight bends they could see the unfortunate riders of the middle section rubbing their eyes as the flecks of unburnt coal peppered them from above. They would look like sweeps by the time they got to the top. Byron made a mental note to thank Marta for allocating him this prime spot when she got back from wherever she had gone. Where had she gone? Probably cuddled up with the elusive Huw somewhere, all her volunteering plans jettisoned. He felt annoyed but also glad for her – she deserved happiness. He suppressed a twinge of jealousy.

The evening air was calm, the sky still light as the train coasted to a stop behind the Power Station. All brakes were applied and for safety's sake many wheels were chocked and Phil gave a final pep talk to the riders. He and his novice recruit would ride the first set down to Rhiw Goch and direct them into the siding. Once arrived he would radio the next ones to ease the brakes off and begin the descent. Every pair of riders had a walkie-talkie and were instructed give the occasional call to say where they were.

'I don't want a running commentary,' Phil explained. 'Just need to know any problems. Besides, you won't hear much once these get going. I'm detached and ready to go. Byron here will uncouple you in turn.' Behind them, Lyd, relieved of her burden, bounced off to Blaenau to refill with water.

Slowly at first but gathering speed, the first four wagons began to trundle back the way they had come. It looked slow, but Byron knew that being low down to the ground and the narrowness of the route made it feel very fast indeed.

Once the wagons had disappeared round the corner, silence descended as quickly as it usually did. Some of the volunteers produced sandwiches, others stretched out on still-warm rocks and chatted.

'I reckon two hours for this lot to be down,' said Byron to no one in particular; 'although if there's any delay we'll be into dusk and we'll have to abandon the rest.'

Thus began the dull bit of the adventure; waiting for the walkie-talkie to crackle and Phil's stentorian tones to declare;

'Okay, send the next pair down. And if I hear whooping, I'll nail their ears to the nearest tree.'

He always said this, and nobody ever took any notice.

'Just back there,' Dylan pointed to the track as it hugged the lakeside and disappeared into the tunnel. 'Too lovely a place to die isn't it?'

Byron nodded. He had been up here when they ran the Santa specials. Although the publicity advertising showed a snow-encrusted winter scene, the reality was often cold, driving rain for the Christmas event. Any serious snow and they'd have had to cancel. But even in the grimmest of conditions, this region was magnificent. A track carved out of the pitiless rock by sheer muscle power and determination to extract the slate from the jagged mountains around. It felt strange to hear whoops and yells in a place stained so indelibly with tragedy and sadness. The same melancholy that had overwhelmed him when he came down from the dam began to creep up on him once more.

This time of year the sunshine took the edge off the bleakness. The rocks lightened in tone as lichen bloomed on their warm surfaces and the heather painted the hillsides a vivid purple. But still it was a desolate, untamed landscape; old, old as time itself, beating to a rhythm of life that was infinitely slower than human lifespan. It was, as Dylan observed, too lovely a place to die.

'I've been thinking,' Byron said. 'That bank account. If there is one, we need to find it.'

'Nothing so difficult as looking for something that might not exist, but come to think…' Dylan's brow furrowed.

'Got an idea?'

He flipped his mobile open and looked at something. 'That string of letters, Sir. Strike you as odd?'

'Go on…'

'No letters above 'I'. 'A to I', apart from a few 'Z's'. If it's a code, it's quite a simple one, but then he's not expecting to have anyone unlock his phone anyway so he doesn't need a complicated encryption.'

'Would you mind telling me what on earth you're going on about?'

'Sorry, yes. Replace each letter with a number and it's the same format as a UK bank account – you know, bank sort code then long account number. Apart from…'

Byron clapped him on the shoulder; 'apart from zeroes which he uses 'Z' for. You clever chap!'

'Well it's an idea. I'll check it when I get in tomorrow. Might not be anything, but you never know.'

'Have you any means of checking now?'

He mused, flipping his phone cover open and shut. 'I suppose Chester might have someone manning the phones, I'll give it a try.'

The phone rang and rang, he was about to give up when it was answered.

'That you, Ricky? Dylan here from Porthmadog. Could you do us a favour? I need a bank account running. You will? Cool. Ready?'

He pronounced the numbers and gave the name of the account holder. Byron could only hear half of the conversation so his attention wandered. Whoever Ricky was, he was grumbling about being ready to go home but Dylan persuaded him to reopen his computer and do the search.

'I've copied you in,' Dylan said, snapping his phone shut. 'He'll send a statement of whatever he finds.'

'You're a genius.'

'Of course.'

The time passed slowly. Although the sun was not visible from their side of the mountain they could see the sky was starting to lose its brightness. The fourth set of wagons were released from their wheel chocks and the brakesmen – actually two women on this one yelled in excitement as the heavy set trundled forward.

'Penny for 'em, Sir?'

Byron started. He'd been trying to assimilate the latest material on Coles. He had put his name to a report that, apart from a few ambiguities, directed the reader to the conclusion that John Coles had shot himself.

Supposing that this string of letters was indeed a cypher to a hidden bank account and that was loaded with cash? Would that change his mind? Well yes. It would remove one of the potent reasons for suicide. But…

Money couldn't buy love. How often had he blessed the wonderful day in which Marlene Fox's interest in him had become clear. When they met he had been scrimping and saving for a house deposit and working hard to make ends meet so she clearly hadn't fallen for his financial status. Love was intangible, sometimes fleeting, but left to ripen as enduring as the mountains above him. A life without love… a life like that of the man who had died only a few hundred yards from here had been living.

In his mind he visualised a pair of weighing scales. On one balance pan the evidence for suicide, on the other for unlawful killing.

He ran them round and round his mind, assigning them a level of importance. Motive, means, opportunity. It all hinged on that gun. Why had so little powder residue transferred itself to Coles' hand? The scales tipped slightly towards foul play, but…

How could anyone remove a gun from the victim's backpack and shoot him with it when all the time the victim was sitting there? No drugs, no knockout blow. Furthermore the door had been locked and when he had glimpsed Coles at the halfway station the window had been shut. Of that he was sure. It had been raining hard and an open window would have attracted his attention.

The scales tipped back to suicide. But where was the other phone?

'1000 to bring it down at 10.' Like a head-worm, the phrase ate into his thoughts.

What on earth had Coles been up to?

Dylan was inspecting his mobile. 'C'mon Ricky…' he muttered. 'D'you know what, I might just go back into work after this and see what else we can dig out on Johnny lad. You want to come as well?'

Byron weighed up the options. It was fish and chip night for him, but no reason why they shouldn't make it another working supper to settle this case one way or the other.

'I might just do that.' He said. The walkie-talkie crackled. 'How's things, Phil?'

'Just you two left, mate. Everyone else down okay. You lead and what's-his-name can go at the back. Take it nice and easy.'

'Will do, Phil.'

'How many times have you done this?' Dylan wanted to know as Byron whipped out one of the wedges from under the wheels.

'Hold the brake,' Byron called as he crossed the track and kicked the other wooden block out. The carriages wouldn't move at once – the incline was barely discernible. But once moving they would gather speed inexorably. The brakesman's job was to anticipate the acceleration and hold the speed down. Gradient markers along the track would warn them of the steepest sections. He threw the wedge into the wagon and grinned as he saw Dylan straining against the brake lever.

'Don't give yourself a hernia, I'll tell you when you need to really pull on that. If we get this right you'll hardly have to strain yourself.' He rubbed the dirt off his hands. 'The answer to your question is six times to date. This will be my seventh. We usually do it on a Bank Holiday weekend or special. Everyone dresses in Victorian costume; stovepipe hats, britches, miners' outfits with pickaxes and so on. Lot of fun.'

Beneath them with a soft rumble the wagons began their love affair with gravity; a slow flirtation at first accompanied by a muted thud as they crossed the rail joints.

'Best bit if we do the whole track,' reflected Byron, having to raise his voice as the noise and jolting increased, 'is the last bit. We have to get up a good head of speed passing the Boston lodge workshops otherwise we don't make it across the Cob. But that's quite a sharp bend. Overcook it and we're off the rails. Too slow and all the anoraks with their fancy cameras fall about laughing as we grind to a halt halfway across. Shame we're not going that far today.'

'Big show is it?' Dylan shouted. The thudding was becoming harsher, like a sledge hammer hitting an anvil rapidly. Although there was no breeze, the flow of air was adding its own note to the noise, cooling the sweat on Dylan's round face.

Byron nodded. 'Attracts a lot of visitors. This is sheer history. It shows the genius of the builders of this railway that they could plan a track with such a long incline. Okay, pull on that brake a bit now.'

Dylan tugged on the brake. The wagons slowed noticeably.

'Ease off. Use the brake to control; you know, stop the speed building rather than slow us down. I've got this brake as well.'

As Byron said this, he felt an uneasy twinge. His brake was sluggish; needing more weight to achieve the same stopping effect than he would have expected. But the brakes had been serviced and probably fitted with new pads so they would need a little time to bed in.

'Bit more on that brake now,' he shouted and to his relief the wagons held their speed. They were approaching Moelwyn tunnel.

'Hope there's no sheep this time!' yelled Dylan as the tunnel walls added their voice to the cacophony.

'Lamb chops all round if there are;' Byron felt exuberant, remembering his first go-kart built out of his brother's old pram wheels. That had had a brake lined with bits of old wellington boot that slammed into the rear wheels. Crude but effective. Unlike this brake.

'Bit more on yours,' he shouted as they emerged from the tunnel. Dylan obeyed and the wagons held their speed. 'We need to keep the speed down for the spiral.'

The dark trunks of the oak trees lining the track raced past. Sheep, fortunately on the other side of the fence, watched them for a few moments then bolted in panic across the fields as they had no doubt done for every wagon that went past. The flow of cool, evening air on his face was pleasant but it could not stop a cold sweat forming above his eyes.

'Bit more on that brake, Dylan!'

His companion heaved on the lever and their speed remained constant. This was a good bit; the huge curve of the Loop built to raise the modern trackbed high enough to squeeze the little line behind the Ffestiniog Power Station. The racket from the wheels and the jolting through their bones was painful but exhilarating. They raced over the bridge and were heading back the way they had come for a short distance before the rails swept round and down to Dduallt halt and merged with the original trackway. Usually locomotives slowed here in case there were passengers waiting, but they had no need or desire to reduce speed. The empty house built right over the marsh on their right and the little stone shelter on the other side flashed past, the sound battering back from the masonry as they entered the straight under the bridge they had just crossed.

'Okay, ease her back a bit!' Byron cried. The gradients and curves were sharper from here on down, and the trackway clung to a ledge that dropped sharply to steep wooded slopes. He hauled on his own brake with all his strength but it seemed to have little effect. The wagons were gathering speed noticeably now, the noise and rush of the air rising in volume.

'Haul back!' Byron felt a spike of irritation. Ahead the trees adjacent the track were casting deepening shadows across the way. But they were approaching much too fast. 'Come on, Dylan, I'll have Phil on my back if we go too fast!'

He turned round. Dylan was pumping the brake handle.

'Not like that!' he yelled. 'Just hold it on.' He pulled back even harder on his brake but what effect it had seemed to have diminished.

'It's not doing anything!' Dylan's face, flickering in the shadows, was set in a horrified mask. 'It was okay just now, but something…'

'Something what?' Byron's guts lurched.

'Snapped off. It was fine one minute, then it went loose.' He shook the lever frantically.

Byron pressed the call tone button on his walkie-talkie. 'Phil, come in. We got problems.'

Normally, Phil Braithewaite's measured tones would instil calm into him, but Phil was down there, he was up here with who knew how many tons of slate threatening to run out of control.

'What's up, Byron?'

'We got brake problems…'

'Slow down, I can barely hear you.'

Byron forced himself to speak clearly and slowly. 'We're one brake down…'

'You only need one. Just take it slower.'

'That brake's not holding well either.'

Phil knew Byron too well to question his assessment. There was a pause. Byron could see the remote cottage of Coed-y-Bleiddiau hurtling up on his right.

'You there, Byron?'

'Just about.'

'You've got a working brake but it's not very good, yeah?'

'Yeah!' Byron gasped. The trucks were starting to sway.

'Your friend, he looked fairly strong. See if he can use his muscle on the working one. And you… can you hear me?'

'Just about…'

'What ballast have you?'

'Slate and a water tank.'

'Right, throw as much out as you can. Ditch the water, get the weight down.'

'Okay, thanks Phil.'

'Leave the walkie-talkie on.'

'Will do.'

Dylan had stopped dragging the brake arm up and down and was peering over the side.

'Get your head in!' screamed Byron. 'Next tunnel is tight!'

With barely a second to spare Dylan threw himself back and the runaway wagons thundered into Garnedd tunnel; an example of 'zero clearance' engineering. Almost as soon as it had gone in, it shot out into the twilight again.

'Come here!' Dylan looked at Byron, his face stony. 'Get down here, I need you to do this brake.'

The brake was starting to slip badly now. The heavy wagons surging forward, accelerating eagerly into the gradient that led to the station at Tan y Bwlch. Dylan clambered over the slate, stumbling and very nearly falling off as the wagons veered sharply to the left. Tan y Bwlch station, picturesque, tranquil and a haven for trainspotters was behind them in seconds. By a dint of crawling and pulling himself along the slates, Dylan reached him at the front.

'What's the matter with your brake?'

'Don't know. It holds but I need you to pull it.' Byron was conscious of the lie. This brake was barely functioning. How fast were they going? He had no idea. The roaring, jolting, barely checked progress of their transport was terrifying. It could only end one way – too fast round a sharp bend and they would be thrown headlong into whatever lay below. Even now the swaying was lifting the wagon's wheels off the track. Dylan braced himself against the metalwork and hauled back on the inefficient brake. His muscles stood out on his arms and he was yelling to himself. The walkie-talkie crackled.

'How much water in the tank?' Phil wanted to know.

'Half-full.' As he said it, Byron thought; *'At the last it's proved I'm an optimist!'*

'Ditch it first. Otherwise it'll slop around and derail you. There's a big bung at the bottom, can you unscrew it?'

Tan y Bwlch woods fled past, the track winding around from side to side. The swaying became harsher and the jolting was sending excruciating pains up Byron's spine.

The water tank was at their end. It was translucent plastic with a capacity of close on two cubic metres of water. It had a large drain hole at the side sealed with a plastic manhole on a screw thread. Two flanges provided a hand grip to tighten and release the bung. Almost certainly a lever had been used to tighten it up and it was blocked by a crate, but Byron was determined to try. He grabbed handfuls of slate from the crate and threw them into the darkness, clearing enough to drag it aside.

'Whatever you're doing, hurry up!' screamed Dylan from up the front. An acrid burning smell came from the tortured brake pads. Byron lashed out with his foot at the flanges on the bung, missing them entirely the first time, but the second blow caught a flange and he felt sure it turned.

'This is hardly holding!'

'Keep trying, anything's better than nothing at all.'

The noise of the wagon had reached battlefield proportions. The machine-gun *thud, thud, thud* of the wheels against the expansion joints in the rails; the grinding of the brakes and the jolting, swaying roar of released energy as gravity fought the brakes and began to win.

Another vicious kick and the bung shifted half a turn and water began to seep around the sides. Byron threw his arms around the tank for support and squatted down. Using his fingers he twisted the bung until all at once, with a gushing flood of greenish water it discharged its contents over the wagon floor and onto the track. Without pausing to watch, Byron grabbed armfuls of slate from the crates. The edges were sharp and his hands became smeared with blood, but he feverishly seized more and lobbed it out of the wagon.

'Phil says the track's clear!' Dylan bellowed, waving the walkie-talkie at him.

'Hold that brake!' he screamed back. 'Try and stop us getting faster.' But looking at the rest of the slate in their wagon and the full wagons behind he was aware of the futility of the remark. Down to Penrhyn the track was at its steepest. The brake was not holding enough to stop them accelerating. The track may well be clear but the thought of this runaway leviathan careering all the way to the end just didn't bear thinking about. By the time they passed the sidings at Rhiw Goch, if not long before, they would be going so fast that the whole contraption would leave the tracks. If it did this further down it endangered homes and possible onlookers.

'Give me that,' he gesticulated to Dylan. The walkie-talkie was thrust into his hand and Dylan resumed his efforts on the brake.

'Phil, listen carefully.' Without waiting for a reply, he went on; 'we've just passed the duck tank.' The galvanised water tank in the woods with a growing family of plastic ducks snapped past them in a blur and fled into the darkness behind. 'We can't hold the speed down. Have they cleared that pile of brushwood from the bottom of Rhiw Goch yet?'

'Not yet. You going to make a leap for it?'

'Anything's better than staying on.'

'It's high but I can't think of another plan. Ambulances and the rest are on their way. Good luck.'

'Thank heaven for Phil's common sense!' thought Byron as he dropped the receiver to the sodden floor. Anyone else might have argued, cast doubt, suggested something impractical. This was a handcart to hell and their best hope was out of it. He joined Dylan who was gasping, fighting to hold back panic.

'We've got to jump.'

'Are you crazy?'

'No choice, Dylan, you got to trust me. When I say go, you go, okay?'

It was too dark to see the doubt in his eyes. 'The walls are too high,' he choked. 'We'll kill ourselves.'

'Not if we jump when I say. There's a pile of scrub further down we can hit. But if we stay on we'll both be crushed when it goes over.'

The wagons lurched and for one moment seemed about to leave the tracks but they crashed back onto the rails. The impact threw them both on the floor and with no one operating the brake gravity triumphantly took over. Their speed began to rise quickly and the swaying of the wagons increased, like a caravan snaking on a motorway.

'Get up on top of these crates,' Byron was aware that Dylan was almost paralysed with shock. 'Hold on and face this way like me.' He was hoarse from yelling over the racket but Dylan understood. Together they crouched, gripping the side rail of the wagon. Byron could see the viaduct of Rhiw Goch with its low walls a short distance ahead. There were lights, people standing around.. *'Oh please don't let them be anywhere near the track...'*

Just ahead the ground dropped away sharply on both sides as the track launched itself onto the magnificent high viaduct. To their right the forestry workers had been clearing undergrowth and thinning the trees out. The waste wood and brambles were piled high at the bottom of the valley, visible only as a black mass. The curve was gentle but their speed manic and the rocking of the wagons had reached a critical level. It was only a matter of time...

The carriages beneath them suddenly convulsed.

'GO!' Byron screamed.

CHAPTER 9

'YOU BACK WITH US, MATE?'

Byron looked at the speaker uncomprehendingly. His face was familiar.

'Talk to me, Byron. D'you know who I am?'

Byron managed a weak smile. 'Phil. Are we good to go yet?'

Phil Braithewaite's thin face creased in a grin. 'You went, mate. You put on the best show I've ever seen. It's all over Facebook, you and that copper friend of yours flying through the air. As if that wasn't enough, the wagons chose that moment to upend and punch through the wall. Hell of a mess, I tell you.'

'Tell me when you want us to go.'

He laughed and Byron sank back into something soft and warm. Something as far removed in discomfort from a steel slate wagon as it was possible to get. Confused recollections swirled around his brain. A harsh, nightmarish journey, shouting, straining to control their vehicle, then a headlong flight...

'What happened?'

'Some low-life tampered with your wagon, that's what. And if I ever get my hands on them...'

Little by little Byron pieced the account together. Suddenly he sat up in bed.

'Dylan! Is he all right?'

'He's in worse shape than you, mate. They've taken him to Bangor with neck injuries and broken ribs. He bounced off the pile of wood and rolled into a tree. You hit it square on. I tell you what, someone is looking after you. When I saw you go, you quite literally did a somersault; I was expecting to see body bags coming up from that gully.'

'Dylan's in Bangor..?'

'Took the ambulance crew an hour to get him out. They were afraid he'd broke his back. They hardly gave you a look in though.

You were wandering around talking rubbish and making a pain in the neck of yourself.'

It took several patient attempts before Byron understood what had taken place. Their runaway wagon had left the rails moments after they abandoned it, smashing through a wall and scattering its remaining cargo across the wooded floor.

'The brakes didn't work, I couldn't slow it down.'

'I checked those wagons myself.' Phil growled. 'Even so, worst case I would allow for one brake to go soft, but not two on the same wagon... No, some scumbag mucked about with them. First thing tomorrow I'm going to take a shufti if they'll let me near.'

'Where am I?'

'Porthmadog. The hospital just outside town. They X-rayed you. Bruised ribs but no broken bones; you'll be feeling sorry for yourself a while.'

'And Dylan...?'

'He's in Bangor, Intensive Care.'

And so it went on, each retelling of the story bringing Byron a little more information that he could retain before some of it leaked away again.

'Is the slate wagon okay?'

'Er, no. I think we'll have to put that in our black museum.'

A nurse interrupted them. 'Some pain relief, Mr Unsworth. They're strong so no driving and certainly no alcohol. We're keeping you overnight to monitor for concussion. If you're okay you can go tomorrow morning.'

'I don't need them,' Byron said when she had gone.

Phil chuckled, reading the label on the box of tablets. 'Oh I think you will! These'll make you woozy.'

'I need to go. I want to see where we crashed.' He swung his legs over the side of the bed and let out a yell as spasms of pain enfolded him.

'Told you!' His companion snorted. He held something up. Byron tried to focus on it. 'Your phone. It fell out when you landed.

I hope you don't mind but your good lady has been trying to ring you.'

'Marta? She's back?'

He looked at Byron narrowly. 'Last time I recall, your wife was called Marlene. Unless you've been a bad boy?'

'Sorry, I meant Mart… Marlene.' Byron shook his head. He felt wretched.

'Hope you don't mind but I took her call for you. I said you'd fallen off a wagon. Told her not to worry, no serious injuries but that you weren't making much sense so she'll call back in the morning.'

'Thanks.'

'Well I'm off to get a bite to eat. My mobile number's on this piece of paper. If you need anything, let me know. When they let you out, give me a ring and I'll pick you up.'

'Thanks.' He repeated. 'Thanks Dylan.'

Phil snorted with laughter. 'Time you had your meds,' he said. 'Doctor Braithewaite orders a little something to chase it down with.' He produced a hip flask and poured a generous slug of spirits into the paper cup the nurse had left.

'I thought she said no alco… alcol…' Byron protested weakly. Phil grinned.

'She would, wouldn't she? But I promise you you'll feel just great with these in you. Drink up and I'm out of here.'

The whisky scorched his mouth, but helped him to swallow the tablets. Every move was painful so Byron fell back into the sheets and looked around him. He was in a small side room. Outside, figures passed, shadows on the window in the door. He could hear someone arguing, then silence fell. Slowly, like retrieving photographs that had spilled onto the floor he relived the experience of a few hours back.

Dylan's brake had abruptly failed. His had not been good from the start. But Phil Braithewaite was a meticulous engineer. How could he have messed up so comprehensively? Sabotage seemed the obvious answer, but was it just vandals being imaginative or deliberately aimed at him? He knew better than to get paranoid. Investigating crimes made enemies, but it was rare for anyone to dare to try to injure or kill a police officer. But the event following hard on the heels of John Coles' 'suicide' was too big a coincidence to pass by.

Then too there was Marta's warning; *'Byron, love, I'm worried. For you, I mean.'* At least he thought it was Marta but it seemed too familiar for her. No, it was Marlene, although what she was worried about he couldn't recall. The longer he thought about it, the less important it seemed. Ten minutes later he could barely remember what had happened or where he was.

It was the strangest dream, except that it was not like a dream. When he closed his eyes, the visions unrolled like a cinema screen; clear and precise. But usually dreams had an annoying habit of stopping when he became aware he was dreaming. But this one was there for the asking. He just had to close his eyes and the movie resumed. When he opened his eyes again, he could recall every detail.

The winding road from Tanygrisiau to Stwlan Dam twisted its torturous way upwards. Around the bend but not yet visible the dark masonry of the dam itself. Byron turned around and the road was quite suddenly below him, as though he had arrived in no time at all. Above him the dam loomed, misshapen goblin guards of Mordor patrolling its rim. The road was guarded but there was another way up. The great buttresses at their steep angle to the ground invited him to climb. Byron looked up the vast expanse of brickwork to the top and knew just what to do. He hitched on his rucksack and walked straight up the impossible incline. It was so easy he couldn't see why anyone else didn't do it. Both sides of him the recessed arches fell away to the ground below. By now he was almost at the point where their upper curve of the arches began, just below the top road.

When he climbed over the wall, the guards had melted away. Only Marta was there, in her shorts. He found himself admiring her legs over and over again. She smiled;

'Would you like a drink, Mr Coles?' In her hand was a silver hip flask. Byron tried to say; 'I'm not Mr Coles, but she just kept smiling in an infuriating manner, displaying even, white teeth.

'Do have a drink,' she said sweetly. 'It will make things so much easier for us.'

'You know I have a gun,' he heard himself protest. She just kept smiling and offering him the flask.

'It's here, in my rucksack. I have a gun. You understand?'

'So have we, Mr Coles. But it's too late now.'

'What do you mean too late?'

'Look over there, in the water.' She skipped lightly onto the wall and pointed down. Deep below a light flickered up through the ripples. A dark shape, like a small submarine, moved beneath the water, nudging at the wall.

'When will it go off?' It was funny, thought Byron, how John Coles just knew what it was. Perhaps that was what explosive experts did – they just knew a bomb when they saw one.

Marta threw her head back and laughed, a strangely merry laugh. 'Look,' she pointed across the lake.

Twenty metres or so from the wall a huge whirlpool had formed. Before his eyes it grew until the vortex was tearing at the dam wall. Behind him a hissing sound, like a locomotive boiler about to eject its safety plugs. He turned and looked down from the dizzying height. Below a curtain of spray jetted from the dam face, blasting hundreds of metres out across the mountainside.

'Too late,' Marta crowed.

Within an impossibly short time, the crack had opened wide enough for the water to prise its fingers into the gap. With a rumble a large chunk of masonry fell out and the curtain of water had turned into a spout that rocketed across the valley. Rainbows danced in its wake. Marta was still laughing and continued to laugh as yet more dam wall collapsed. The road beneath their feet buckled, rose and then slipped downwards into a dark aperture into which the funnel of water was racing.

He turned and ran to the highest spot and watched with a kind of detached horror as Stwlan dam fell in on itself. The noise was thunderous, the mountain beneath his feet shook and the rocks above bounced and careered down the steep slopes into the rapidly-emptying lake.

Then he was running. Absurdly racing ahead of the titanic inundation that was pouring from the shattered dam. Running past Tanygrisiau and along the track until he was in Blaenau Ffestiniog station.

He boarded the train, and tried to tell the guard that the dam had ruptured but the guard just kept pestering him for his ticket. Marta was there too, still smiling.

'Not this carriage, Mr Coles. This is reserved.'

She led him up the platform until they came to the tiny, green carriage at the end. He tried the doors, they were locked.

'We keep it locked,' she murmured. 'But I'll open it for you.' He climbed in and settled himself and she wrapped her hands around his arm and placed her head coyly on his shoulder. Her silver-blonde hair ran down his chest. 'Let me fetch you a drink.'

'No time,' he said, pulling himself away. 'The train has to leave now.'

Then she was gone. He caught sight of her bizarrely flapping a flag at the end of the platform. At first he thought she was despatching the train, but realised she was signalling in semaphore. To whom? He hardly seemed to care. Nothing mattered now. He was about to die. In twenty minutes his life would be over. The water from Stwlan dam was stripping all buildings, trees, roads and villages off the face of the earth as it exulted in its long-sought freedom. But John Coles cared nothing for that either. He looked around the small, homely carriage, then through the windows and said to himself, *'it's too lovely a place to die.'*

He sat back in the seat by the window and waited for the moment. The train halted and he could hear sheep frantically bleating up ahead.

'Here it comes,' he thought. Windows opened along the tunnel, noises, shouting, but John Coles closed his eyes and waited for the moment.

There was a sharp click and the key inserted in the lock. The door was swung open and somebody jumped up on the running board. A hard, metal object was pressed against his skull. He sobbed as the trigger was pulled.

Byron sat up in bed. The action made him wince but the strong pain-killers had taken the savage edge off the pain, at least for now. He was sweating and his heart was banging against his bruised rib cage.

It was a dream. No danger of mistaking that weird sequence of events for reality. But he realised what the cocktail of drugs and strong alcohol had done. It had freed his mind to explore the possible truth of what had happened to Coles and why. Disregarding the surreal elements all the detached details were there, fitted together into an outrageous, horrific whole.

For a few minutes he tried to talk himself out of it. No one in their right mind takes a course of action directed by a mixture of opioid painkillers and whisky. He was in that darkest hours of the night frame of mind when the smallest problems were amplified out of all proportion. In the morning he would laugh at his stupidity. He might tell Marlene, but then again he might not. But he was certainly not going to do anything right now. He was about to turn over and try to sleep when he saw his phone had a message. Clumsily he logged in.

Not only were his fingers not cooperating, but his eyes slipped around the tiny screen. It was copied in from Ricky's reply to Dylan.

'Got it! Took a while because he deliberately spelled his name wrong. But if Jon Colles is your man, this is his account summary.'

The attached file took a few moments to open. When it did, Byron's eyes watered. The account had been opened two years ago. Since then five sums, each in excess of forty thousand pounds had been deposited.

Ricky had added a note. *'Money originated from Eastern Europe. This smells bad!'*

Byron almost laughed. It stank.

'Dylan, that you?'

'No it's not. It's Phil Braithewaite. Byron, are you seriously phoning me for a chat at half three in the morning?'

'Sorry, Phil. I need your help.'

'You're having a laugh. Go back to sleep.'

'Phil, this won't wait. You got to get down here. I need to be somewhere.'

'No!'

'If you hang up I'll call back.'

'No problem, you'll be blocked. Now get some sleep and I'll drop by in the morning.'

'Phil, this is deadly serious.'

'So am I. I've got to take a track crew up first thing tomorrow to see what damage you clowns did to our railway and I need to sleep.'

'Phil, please…'

A heavy sigh. Then; 'okay, what do you want?'

Byron told him.

'No, no and thrice no! You're drugged up, concussed and you've knocked back a healthy portion of single malt. I hoped it might make you sleep, clearly I was wrong. If you think I'm going to take you seriously, you're sadly mistaken.' The line went dead.

It took Byron a few moments to realise what had happened. He pummelled his phone keyboard but he couldn't easily coordinate his fingers. At last it rang again.

'This had better be good!' Phil was positively grinding his teeth.

'I promise you it is. A thousand to bring it down at ten. I thought it was a money thing…'

'What the hell are you going on about? You were shouting that at everybody earlier.'

Byron tried to clear his head. He had a bad feeling that Phil was going to hang up again.

'It's not money, Phil, it's weight. A thousand pounds or kilograms of explosive at ten metres below the water level. And Phil, Marta's involved.'

He laughed sourly. 'Marta or Marlene? You didn't seem too sure which earlier.'

'I know I'm not making much sense at the moment….'

'You're telling me!'

'Phil, I really need you to help me.'

'Tell me again what crazy wild-goose chase you want me to join you in and why.'

Byron told him.

There was a long silence. Then Phil said; 'so let's get this straight. You want me to fetch you out of there, then drive us up to Stwlan dam to see if anyone has propped a bomb up against it?'

'That's about it.'

'You're mad. I'm never giving anyone else my number after this.'

'Phil,' Byron felt woozy again and sweat was breaking out in his armpits. 'If I'm wrong you can laugh at me for years. You have my permission never to let me forget it. But if I'm right, could you live with yourself? This could be the terrorist routage of the century.'

'You mean outrage?'

'Will you come?'

Byron chafed at the time it took for Phil to arrive. He tried asking himself, '*if this was a planned terrorist attack, what would be the best time to maximise damage and inconvenience?*'

The answer was when the water in the top dam was at its peak, ready to rush down to turn the turbines for the morning surge. When would that be? About five? The overstretched power grid would signal for the station to deliver its massive gigawatt boost but nothing would be forthcoming. Instead a trail of death and devastation down the Maentwrog valley and the news story of the decade. Who would benefit? The immediate answer would be the dam protesters. A blown dam would be hardly the best incentive to investors to build more hydro-electric schemes. But there had to be more to it than that. This had been in planning for at least two years.

In a bid to distract himself, he opened his emails on his phone. There were plenty from work, many more spam and unsolicited junk and a few from the railway. One from Sue in the office caught his eye.

'I'm sending you this as Marta is under your wing. I've replied to the Kilroys for the moment, but you might need to find out what really happened.'

Attached was a screen shot of the customer feedback form. Evan and Sally Kilroy and their two toddlers were airing their grievance about last Saturday evening's train ride.

'... the children particularly wanted to travel in the little green carriage at the back. Thomas has drawn pictures of it and given it a name. So it was more than a little irritating to be told it wasn't available when someone was sitting in it so it clearly was in use. The member of staff who was called Marta was abrupt, rude and would not listen even though we assured her the children would be fine in there. In the end we moved because she insisted…'

Byron screwed his face up and exhaled heavily, trying to get to grips with this. Marta was involved. He had known that for some time even if he had been unable to admit it. But he had been blinded by his paternal attitude towards her. Poor, lonely Marta Kowalczyk had run rings around him with her apparent distress at discovering the body. Tears, panic attacks, all that drama when they had walked up Moel y Gest – she was a consummate actress. Her anguish had weaselled the information about their enquiries out of him. By pretending to be horrified about suicide, she had effectively interrogated him for all the clues they had amassed pointing to murder. Then there was her flirting and acting like she was in awe of him; Byron almost writhed in embarrassment at the recollection.

Sue had written a few more words at the bottom of the email; *'Byron, I'm sorry to drop this on you but she does look up to you.'*

How many more volunteers and staff were chuckling behind their hands at them both?

Phil Braithewaite's presence was announced by an ongoing argument that could be heard halfway up the corridor.

'Yes, I'm aware of the time, I wish Mr Unsworth was too… No, I wouldn't be here if it wasn't important… No, he doesn't think it will wait until the morning…'

The voices drew nearer.

'He'll have to sign that, I'm not taking responsibility for him. Concussion? I could give him concussion…'

The door burst open and the senior staff nurse strode in with Phil just behind her.

'I heard,' said Byron weakly. 'I'll sign whatever you need me to, but just let me out of here.'

Staff nurse, Naomi Stansted, glared at him. Phil scowled at him. 'Sorry,' Byron said, 'this really can't wait.'

His clothes were arranged on a nearby chair. They were filthy with woodland soil and torn in a couple of places. When Byron tried to stand the room did a somersault around him and he very nearly fell over. The staff nurse and Phil were watching him grimly, waiting for him to see sense or better still pass out.

'Get me the paperwork,' he growled. 'Let me get dressed.'

When they returned he was fully dressed. A scrappy signature was applied to the bottom of a form and Phil led him, or more precisely dragged him, to the waiting car. The night sky was lit by a full moon but the cool air did at least clear his head slightly.

'Where to first?'

Byron looked uneasily at him. He sounded angry. By the glow of the courtesy light he could see he was angry.

'Stwlan dam,' he said, easing himself painfully into the passenger seat of Phil's vintage Mercedes, his pride and joy.

'If it's still there, you mean? Byron, I've known you for most of my life. If it was anyone else I wouldn't be here. But don't you think you might be wrong?'

'I hope I am. I really hope I am. But what if I'm not?'

'Well call the police, then. They can be there in no time.'

'I tried leaving a message with Superintendent Ward. But there's all hell breaking loose across Wales about these dam proposals. They're stretched to the limit.'

'Oh come on! They'll answer 999; they have to, and you can get them up there.'

'Okay, but I guarantee they'll fob us off.'

Byron was right. The emergency services operator kept repeating; 'if this is a matter of immediate life and death, we will send a unit out. But in the circumstances…'

Byron threw caution to the winds. 'Do you know who I am? I am DI Byron Unsworth of Avon and Somerset Force. I have reason to believe a major terrorist attack is imminent.'

She was genuinely apologetic. 'Sir, our nearest armed response unit is in Chester. The nearest helicopter is in Welshpool. But I have a colleague at the moment on the line to the Power Station. We will get someone to you as soon as we can. But can you at least check with the security operatives at Trawsffyndd…?'

'It's not Trawsffyndd!' Byron bellowed. 'It's the peak storage station at Blaenau! Get the areas beneath the dam evacuated!'

'Keep talking,' Phil started the engine and with uncharacteristic haste swung the car out of the hospital and onto the Porthmadog bypass.'

'Are you still there?' Byron cried. 'Can you get me a line to the peak storage at Ffestiniog. NOT Dinorwig,' he added for good measure.

'It's ringing, Sir.' The emergency operator sounded scared. 'I'll put you through. You'd better talk to them.'

It took even longer to persuade the power station security of his concerns. They had CCTV overlooking the top lake; the dam was quiet. No one had been up there. Stop wasting their time. Byron had to pull all the rank he could muster just to get an assurance that they would be given the key to the gate that led up to the dam. Once they were off the line the emergency operator came back on.

'Did you get anywhere, Sir?'

'No I did not. I need you to instigate an emergency evacuation protocol. They must have one. Tell whoever needs to know that we have a possible dam failure. Get them clearing the area.'

He rang off and put his head in his hands.

'What have I done…?' he moaned.

His companion smiled grimly. 'Scrambled North Wales' anti-terrorism unit, sent men with loud-hailers into the streets, banging on people's doors at four in the morning telling them to get the hell out. You'll either be the hero of the hour or…'

He didn't need to finish. If this was a false call, it was out to pasture for DI Unsworth and forget any golden handshake.

Phil's Mercedes swept past Penrhyn. The streets of the sleepy town were utterly deserted. He floored the accelerator and the car bounded forward up the slope towards the Oakley Arms.

Phil was a trained military driver. Even so, Byron had never known him exceed a speed limit. But tonight's driving was unforgettable. After Oakley arms the road to Blaenau swept round in a lazy curve then dropped off to the left sharply. The speedometer barely dropped below seventy and the tyres howled for traction as they rounded two more sharp corners and the road began to rise steadily.

'At least we're not likely to meet anything coming...' Byron thought, pulling his seatbelt tighter. Two hair-raising journeys in one night. He'd better ring Marlene while he still had chance.

He was expecting voicemail, but she was awake and angry.

'Byron, I was about to ring you. Phil said you fell off a wagon...'

'That's true, but Marlene...'

'But nothing! The volunteer group have posted a video. You and someone else flying off Rhiw Goch. I hardly call that just falling off. I'm going to kill Phil when I see him next.'

'He's here with me.'

'Where are you? You sound like you're in a car.'

'Marlene, listen, you got to help us,' Byron's head was starting to spin again.

'No, you listen. I'm surprised you weren't killed. I should have been told.'

'Marlene, will you listen? You were right!'

That did the trick. Marlene fell silent and Byron, clinging to the door handle to avoid being thrown around explained.

'It's major, love. Some group are going to bring down the dam. Coles supplied the explosive in increments and they've got a thousand kilos of high-grade stuff. My guess is he wasn't told what it was for, but he got curious – went up there to do some calculations and knew they had enough to crack the dam wall.'

'Hence the thousand to bring it down...'

'At ten metres depth,' Byron finished for her. 'They saw him and set up this suicide.'

'How?'

'Marta...'

'Ah!' In spite of her fear, she couldn't conceal the satisfaction from her voice. 'Did she kill him?'

'No, impossible, she was with me the entire time we were stuck outside the tunnel, but she made sure he was on his own. I think they expected him to get on at Tanny, but he turned up unexpectedly at

Blaenau and they had to improvise. Once she had locked him in she made sure no one else was with him, phoned or texted ahead and the sheep were driven on to the line. The train stops, perfectly ordinary reason, Coles has no need to be suspicious, then, bang!'

'How did they unlock the door?'

Byron was feeling sick. Phil's car was accelerating up the hill towards Tanygrisiau. He fought back the nausea. 'Easy enough, the key's only a square bit of metal.'

'What about the gun? How did they get hold of it?'

'They didn't. Remember what I told you Janice said? The guns were issued by the mining company in South Africa. There could have been any number of them. So…'

'Identical firearm, so in all probability he was working with an ex-colleague!' she finished. 'Clever! And what about the Gravity Train? Not a coincidence, huh?'

'No, Phil said the brakes had been tampered with.'

'I haven't checked that yet,' warned Phil, but added; 'But I know those brakes were fine the other night.'

They roared over the rise and before them the street lamps of Tanygrisiau glimmered. The whole region bathed in bright moonlight. Quiet.

'Got to go, love.' Byron said. 'We're nearly there. Love you hon.'

'Come back alive, darling.'

Once the line went dead he yelled; 'Why aren't they evacuating? Look at the place! They should be emptying the houses right now.'

Phil, throwing the car into the long drive that led to the power station muttered something inaudible.

At the power station gates, a uniformed security guard was scratching his backside. He swung the gates open and slouched over to the car.

'Yuh wasting your time, pal,' he said, his voice surly. 'Nothing wrong here.' Byron was about to answer when Phil leapt out.

'Stand up straight!' he bawled. 'You will address DI Unsworth as 'Sir' at all times, understood? And you will cooperate with everything he asks you to do? Got that?' His voice echoed off the nearby walls. The man jumped as if he had been shot. Another man emerged from a nearby office.

'Simon, Leave this to me,' he jerked his thumb over his shoulder and with relief the first guard scurried off. 'Come in, gentlemen,' he said. He made little attempt to disguise his scepticism but at least he was civil.

Five minutes later they were looking at the CCTV screen that monitored the top dam.

'How many cameras?' Phil wanted to know. Byron tried to focus but his head was spinning.

'One fixed view over the whole lake, one moveable the other side; another two fixed along the front wall.'

'All working?' Byron asked, tasting bile in his mouth.

He hesitated a moment, then said, 'number three, the moveable that overlooks the far side, the drive motor failed earlier this week. We have a new one on order, but the fixed one is fine.' He tapped the screen.

The blackness of the lake was disturbed only by the flickering of the moonlight on the wavelets. No movement, no shadowy figures, no guards of Mordor. Nothing. Byron felt seriously as if he was about to be ill.

'Anything up there, we'd have seen it,' the guard smiled reassuringly. 'We appreciate your concern, Sir, but on this occasion we really think…'

'The road up to the dam,' Phil interrupted. 'You have a key to the gate?'

'We do, but I assure you…'

'Then get it.'

'Very well, Sir.'

If the journey up to Tanygrisiau was hair-raising, Byron was terrified of the next bit. Phil's car tore out of the compound and hurtled up the steep slope, almost leaving the ground as it bounced over the level crossing. Up past the pool where Byron had talked to the boys and on around the tiny streets of upper Tanygrisiau.

'What have I done?' he kept thinking. *'This is the biggest damn-fool mistake of my life. I'm finished.'* Below them the village slumbered although the sound of the car wakened a dog which began to bark.

'Any moment now we get to the gate. It will be locked, all normal. All quiet.'

Marlene's voice intruded in his private meltdown. *'That CCTV of the lake - it's all too good to be true.'*

'John Coles shot himself.' He argued.

She whispered; *'John Coles had to be killed. He would have blown the whistle. Marta schmoozed up to you to see how much you knew. When you went to the tunnel a second time, they knew you were onto them. That's why they tampered with your wagons.'*

'But we'd concluded suicide…'

'Marta didn't know that.' Marlene whispered deep in his brain. *'Oh, the irony!'*

'Any moment now we'll get to the bottom gate. It will be padlocked. Everything will be normal. Normal. Normal…'

Phil slammed on his brakes and the car almost stood on its nose. The steel gate was in the full glare of the headlights. 'Where's the key?' he asked.

'Here.' Byron held it up and closed his eyes as another wave of sickness hit him. Phil snatched it and bounded from the car. Seconds later he jumped back in.

'That was quick.'

'No padlock. Hold on tight.'

The road ahead, lit by the full moon was a dark band that looked like a black ribbon had been carelessly tossed to the floor. It swerved and squirmed and the car's engine yelled in protest as Phil fought the gears up the crazy incline. Byron hoped he wouldn't vomit – Phil would draw the line at clearing that up from his beloved car. He wound down the window and inhaled the cool night air.

'Still nothing happening down there,' he fretted. Tanygrisiau slumbered on through its silent night.

'Takes time,' Phil reminded him. 'Chain of command, all that stuff. There it is.'

With a final squeal of tyres the car was at the foot of the dam. Black and awful, holding its liquid prisoner until the grid demanded that it be allowed out for its routine exercise. For a moment Byron was back in his weird dream. Perhaps he should defy gravity and walk up the buttress.

Phil gunned the car and they ascended the last few hundred metres to the very top. They were level with the top of Stwlan Dam, looking down on the calm, black water flickering in the moonlight. Everything was absolutely fine. Off to the left the Maentwrog valley basked in moonlight. It was fine. To their right the great basin formed by the dam and the rocky mountain slopes was fine too. Ahead the black massifs of Moelwyn Bach and Moelwyn Mawr looked on impassively.

'Come on,' Phil slammed his door and walked round.

'I'm sorry, Phil. I really thought…'

'Come on. We need to look.'

'I've wasted your time.'

'I'll be the judge of that. Why no padlock on the gate? Let's have a good look round.'

'Probably just forgot to put it back on. You go, I'll stay here.'

Phil loomed over him, a dark shape against the moonlit sky. 'Look, mate, I've probably burnt out a clutch getting up here. If your Marlene thinks something major is planned, that's good enough for me. I'm not going back down until we know for sure.'

'Phil,' Byron faltered. 'Don't make me… I can't go out on there. I'm… I'm afraid of heights.'

The black form regarded him for a few seconds more, then with a grunt turned away. Byron closed his eyes. Wretched didn't even begin to describe how he felt.

He watched Phil stride off toward the dam. Across the top the road, straight as an arrow, was concealed in the moonlight shadow cast by the wall. Afraid he would be sick, Byron climbed out of the car. The painkillers were wearing off; a sharp crushing pain around his rib cage was making breathing difficult and a multitude of bruises were making their presence felt. He gripped the top of the car door for support.

Phil had stopped by a small gantry atop the dam wall on which was mounted a camera. It was not far across but even so a sharp drop down to the base of the dam wall. He climbed up a little way, then prodded before climbing back down again and making his way back to to the car.

'What is it?'

'Something wrong. I'm not an electronics specialist, but I'm guessing that camera is not the one they're seeing back down there.'

'What d'you mean?'

'Come and see.'

His legs hurt fiercely. The exertion made him gasp for breath and his ribs protested. Byron drew near to the gate that blocked the road across the dam.

'Don't look down.' Phil's voice had become gentle. He coaxed Byron to climb on to the wall to get past the gate and supported him as they walked along the roadway to the camera. He glanced at Byron's stricken face. 'Just look straight ahead.'

Byron did so, trying to forget the thousands of tons of water on one side and the immense void in the other. His belly heaved and he felt the solid floor beneath him begin to sway. The gantry that looked tiny from back by the car now loomed over them. He felt even worse when Phil scrambled up and began climbing the metalwork.

'Here,' Phil said. 'Someone's been a bit clever.'

The cable from the camera had been cut. But a small connector had been fitted from which another cable disappeared around the side of the gantry. Phil reached with his fingers, leaning out over the void. Byron kept his eyes fastened on the road until he heard him say;

'Got it!'

He sprang down and held out the object. It was a smartphone. On its screen was a video of the moonlit surface of Llyn Stwlan playing and two views of the front wall of the dam.

'Patched in..?'

Phil nodded. 'All three could have been recorded simultaneously any bright moonlit night. Then when they needed to cover their activities they shoved it into the camera feed. After damaging the other camera first.'

'So that they wouldn't be able to control it and change the view. So there is likely to be something here.'

'I owe you an apology, Byron. I should have known you wouldn't create such a fuss otherwise. So we need to find whatever they've rigged up here.'

'A thousand at…'

'Ten metres. Yes I know that off by heart as well now.'

'Middle of the wall, ten metres down. And a lot of it.' *Supposing his dream of a huge bomb shaped like a submarine was true, what hope would they have of getting it out?*

Phil strode off further along the road. Byron followed, every step increasing his anxiety. It was just so high up here! He stumbled behind, his eyes locked on the far side. Ahead Phil was kneeling on the road halfway across, pulling at something.

'This is it,' he said quietly.

A short length of scaffold pole lay on the road, flat against the wall. It looked discarded except for one odd feature. In the middle of the pole were a number of loops of rope, coiled tightly around the pole. They were the ends of lengths that disappeared through a small aperture in the wall left there to allow rainwater to soak away into the lake.

'Help me,' Phil grunted, pulling the end of the pole away from where it was snuggled tightly against the bottom of the wall. But even their combined strength could not move it far, and when they released it, it snapped back firmly against the wall.

'Five pieces of rope,' Phil said. 'Two hundred kilos on the end of each. It'll need both of us to get these up.'

'Can't we just cut them? If they sink to the bottom they'll be less effective.'

'Do you want to chance it?' Byron couldn't see his eyes, but his voice supplied the answer.

Phil reached over the wall, straining to grab the rope that disappeared into the pitch-black water. Finally he had a hand hold and threw his body weight back onto the road whilst Byron hauled on the line. It was quite thin rope and being wet slipped through his fingers and cut into his sore palms.

'C'mon,' Phil urged, straining his muscles to haul the weight up from the deep. Little by little it came, bumping and rolling against the dam face and increasing in weight as the water pressure decreased.

'After three; one... two...three..!' Byron's torn tendons sent spasms of pain through him as the weight was dragged up and surfaced in the shadow of the wall. It took all their combined strength to heave it on to the top of the wall.

'Steady... We need to lift it down.'

It was a squat, plastic barrel about a metre diameter and just over a metre long enclosed in a net to which the rope was tied. It was sealed and featureless. Just a big, bulky barrel of explosive. They lowered it gingerly to the road surface and looked at it as water ran blackly off it and across the tarmac.

'Now what?' Byron said.

'You just throw it back,' said a voice behind them.

CHAPTER 10

MARTA HELD THE GUN at arm's length in both hands. The muzzle shook. Her face was in shadow but it was clear she was tense.

'Throw it back,' she repeated.

'Or what?' Demanded Phil.

'I shoot you. I shoot you both.' The gun muzzle twitched.

'Why?' Byron asked.

'Isn't it obvious? This dam must be brought down. Now put that barrel back or I will kill you.'

'You're not a killer, Marta,' Phil said.

'No, but there's a first time for everything.'

'This is the worst combination,' Byron realised. She was resolved to see this through and that desperation could induce her to commit murder. He had to keep her talking.

'Why do you want the dam down?'

'I'm surprised you ask. Don't you see the way this land has been abused? Mined, flooded, quarried, treated as a resource to be raped then discarded. There are people who love this country. They grew up in valleys where their families lived for generations. But soon those valleys will be turned into huge lakes to keep the greedy English in power. Is this any way to treat a nation? With this dam down, they'll have to rethink.'

'It's funny how articulate she has become, all of a sudden,' Byron thought. All that pausing to query an unfamiliar phrase or stumbling to find the right words. Now this fluency - Marta had been putting it all on for their benefit.

'Is this Marta speaking,' he asked, 'or Huw?'

'Ah! Huw, my faithless lover. Did he make you jealous, Byron. Did you have hopes yourself?'

'Never mind that, just answer the question. Does Huw belong to some activists looking for Welsh rule? I want to know why you're doing this.'

'He is one of the sons of Glyndŵr,' she pronounced impressively. 'You know of them?'

Byron and Phil exchanged looks and shrugged. Neither could honestly say they had heard of this group, but splinter organisations with an axe to grind sprung up seemingly overnight.

'So Huw sang you the songs of the old Welsh, the days of freedom and valour and got you to do his dirty work for him?' Phil said with ill-concealed contempt. 'I never had you down as stupid.'

'Don't call me that!' She had turned so that the moonlight illuminated her face. Her mouth was slightly open, the crooked teeth picked out by its light. 'You're the stupid ones, especially...' she turned to face Byron, 'especially you! Did you like my shock and distress? How I trembled and wept and held onto you like I needed you! I knew your wife is an invalid; I needed to know what you guessed and you gave it to me in exchange for nothing more than a shy embrace, a little sign of affection. Oh you were stupid! You held nothing back. I thought you would ask for more but you made it so easy.'

'You didn't have to try and kill us!' Byron exploded.

'But we had to, surely you see that? You were too thorough for your own good. We gave you so many reasons to think Mr Coles took his own life, but you had to go on looking for something else.'

'How did you sabotage the wagon?' Phil demanded.

She smiled. 'It was Huw's idea. He greased the front brake so it would slip, then cut the split pin at the back so the brake would work for as long as the rest of the pin stayed in place. When it fell out the brake would fail. We knew that by then you would be going too fast to stop.'

'Yeah, yeah. You were so clever,' Phil cut in. 'But what makes you think you haven't been used too?'

'What do you mean?'

'This lot;' he gestured towards the barrel and over the side of the dam. 'What time do you think it's due to go off?'

'Why should I tell you that?'

'Because I think you've been told the wrong time.'

She was silent for some time. The gun was trembling violently now. 'It will explode at seven this morning,' she said finally.

'No it won't. It will go off long before then. And Huw told you to wait up here, did he? To make sure no one came up to investigate.'

'When will it explode?' She asked, her voice harsh.

'Very soon, by my reckoning.'

'You're lying. Each barrel has a timer inside. They are all set for seven o' clock. How can you know otherwise?'

'Recognise this?' Phil reached inside his jacket. She twitched the gun at him. 'Oh come on, Marta, I'm hardly going to pull a gun on you, am I?'

He held out the mobile phone he had removed from the camera gantry.

'Yes, we recorded the lake and copied it onto that phone. But that doesn't tell you when the timers will go off.'

'It doesn't,' agreed Phil. 'But when the video runs out, even those goons in the power station will notice something's wrong, won't they? So I deduce that your boyfriend has arranged that around about when this video finishes, the bomb will detonate.'

'How long left on the video?' Byron asked, his heart sinking.

'Fifteen minutes.'

'You're lying,' Marta repeated faintly.

'Did you see him set the timers?' Byron demanded. Phil butted in before she could answer;

'Believe me or not, it's your funeral;' he shrugged. 'But what a risk to take! From what I understand about this Huw character, he wouldn't make a mistake like that. What time did he tell you to get away from here?'

'Five o' clock,' Marta was biting her fingertips now. Dylan's habit seemed to be catching.

Byron laughed bitterly. 'It's four forty-five now. Huw's used you, Marta. And now you're used up he's disposing of you.'

Phil turned back to the wall. 'So now that's cleared up, I intend to try and save this dam.'

'Take another step and I will fire.' Marta's voice was shaking, with fear or anger, it wasn't easy to tell.

'No you won't,' Phil Braithewaite turned away and flung himself over the wall to fumble for another of the ropes that secured the barrels. 'This isn't you, Marta. You know better than to do something so stupid.'

'I told you not to to call me stupid!' She cried.

'Then don't behave stupidly... Got it!' Phil grunted and his body swung back down so that he was standing on the road. 'Give me a hand with this,' he said, passing the second line of rope across to Byron.

'Marta, Phil's right,' Byron fastened his eyes on her face – it helped him forget his vertigo - and held out his hand to her. 'You're way out of your depth and Huw cheated you. But there's still time to get out. Don't make things worse, just drop the gun and help us save the dam.'

She backed away. 'Do you just think I'm a stupid Polish girl? Is that it? I'm the one who just does as she's told. 'Wipe the tables, Marta, check the doors, fetch us some drinks, Marta.' Don't you realise I can think for myself?'

'Then really think for yourself, will you? You made me feel special, like I mattered to you. Why? Because you wanted to manipulate me. Huw's done the same to you. The news about the dam proposals only came out six months ago but John Coles has been paid for supplying stuff for this bomb for the last two years. So think about it, Marta. Whoever Huw was working with they had been putting this together much longer than they told you.'

'Can you get hold of this?' Phil tugged at the rope and Byron twisted it round his hand and trying to ignore the savage pain in his ribs began reeling the second barrel in.

'Did Huw make you feel special?' Byron's anger was making him reckless. 'Did it cross your mind that when he had his arms round you that he was using you like a tool? Do you really believe he's a Welsh freedom fighter or some such drivel? I guarantee he's been paid to make sure this installation is blown up so that Britain's power supply is brought to its knees. Somebody will make a huge profit from that and you fell for it.'

'You don't know Huw!' She cried. 'He wouldn't do that!'

'Neither do you. Where did you meet him? Travelling across Eastern Europe. Now there's a coincidence. John Coles was dealing with explosive suppliers from Eastern Europe.'

'Here it comes!' Phil shouted. With a wash of water the barrel surfaced. It was identical to the first.

'Two down, three to go!' Phil exulted.

'Still got to get them away from here,' Byron warned. 'Does industrial explosive go off without a detonator?'

'No idea.' Phil replied. 'Marta, use your brain for once. If we throw this over the edge, will it go up?'

There was no answer, Marta was standing rigid, looking out across the valley, muttering ugly sounding Polish words. *'Świnia.* He told me to wait by the base of the dam…'

This time the effort of lifting the barrel over the inner wall sent Byron's bruised rib cage into a spasm of pain that left him crouched on the road gasping for breath. The exertion demanded air but the movement of his lungs fired off crushing pains. A bout of wheezing turned into coughing which doubled him up in pain. The problem was, he couldn't allow himself to cough as each spasm set off fresh waves of agony. Dimly he could see Marta's form walking away, back along the road.

'Marta,' Phil snapped. 'You're going to have to help.'

She spun round and laughed harshly. 'You're giving orders again!'

Phil straightened himself up. 'Look, Marta, I have no idea what Byron here would charge you with, but we've got one unlawful killing of John Coles; that makes you an accessory. Then you and your lover-boy try to maim or kill two serving police officers.

Attempted murder? I'm sure Byron could supply the correct terminology – and now you're about to compound this all by blowing this dam apart and killing a few hundred people down below. You might want to be stupid, but I didn't have you down as cruel. If you cooperate now, at least we can fight your corner.'

'I don't need you to fight my corner,' she choked and turned her back once more.

Byron struggled to stand upright. The coughing had passed, or at least he could suppress it. There seemed only course left open to him. Letting go the rope he limped after her and caught her by the arm. She thrust the gun at him, but he pushed it aside.

'Marta, do it for me.' He wrapped his hands around her slim forearm and pulled her to him.

She was rigid in his grasp. For a moment he thought she might shoot him. Seconds passed during which he sensed a relaxing of her posture; then her weight bore down on him as she slumped, sobbing against him.

'I'm sorry, Byron...'

'Okay, Marta...' he bit his tongue to try to distract himself from the fresh pain that the pressure of her body against his ribs triggered. 'You've been had. We've all been had.' Her face came down on his shoulder and he cradled her head as convulsions shook her slim form.

'Why...?' she moaned.

'I don't know, but we'll find out who really did this. Marta, I can't promise you anything, they'll be a full enquiry. But I will stand up for you, try and help them see you were used, but...'

'We're none of us going anywhere if we don't get this thing out,' Phil cut across. 'Marta, we need you to help. Five minutes left on the video.'

Still sobbing, she turned back and wrapped her hands round the rope. She hauled on it like one possessed, straining and cursing as they hauled the third barrel from its nesting place ten metres down. With the three of them it was easier, although Byron's chest hurt so much he could barely stand and he hunched over the wall, struggling for breath, wondering how the lake suddenly looked so pretty with the wavelets lit by the lowering moon.

The third barrel joined the other two weeping water over the road.

'Can we crack them open?' Phil wanted to know.

'We're better off getting the rest up,' Marta said. She was wet where the barrel had pressed against her and her hands were cut with the thin ropes.

'But if only one goes off, we're in trouble,' Phil's understatement struck Byron as faintly ludicrous. 'If we could get them open and find out exactly when the timer runs out…'

'Let's try this;' Byron fished out his penknife and cut the rope, then rolled the barrel to the other side of the wall and looked out over the parapet. Down below he could see a multitude of flashing blue lights around the village. He closed his eyes as another wave of vertigo added to his woes. Running his fingers under the end of the barrel he stood it upright and heaved it onto the wall.

'No. You fish the rest out,' he waved Phil and Marta back. 'But get down when I say.'

Whether they obeyed or not he didn't wait to find out. He twisted the barrel and gave it a shove. It hung motionless for a moment then dropped out of sight.

'DOWN!' he yelled and the three of them dived for cover. Byron nearly blacked out with the pain.

They heard a muffled thud as the barrel hit the ground but nothing else. When they looked over the parapet, in the moonlight they could see it had buried itself in the marshy soil at the foot of the huge buttress.

'Put the other two further along,' Phil advised. 'If they go off it'll spread the blast out.'

That job fell to Byron. He cut another barrel free and began to roll it along the road, further across the dam. His head was spinning, and he kept his eyes on the thing as it weaved, lumpy in its net vest until he had gone about half the remaining distance to the far side. Once again, almost passing out with the pain he manhandled the awkward thing onto the wall.

'DOWN!' he yelled again as it dropped into the void. He saw the other two throw themselves against the tarmac. This time there was a distant smashing sound but when he peered over the edge it was swallowed up in a shadowy area. He was certain it had broken in pieces. Reassured by this he sent the third barrel over the same place and this time bits of it rolled out into the light. He could see that the barrel had shattered and vomited its contents across a wide area of hard ground.

By now, Marta and Phil were struggling with the fourth canister. When they had it in the road, Phil seized his pocket knife and sawed through the rope; then without waiting for Byron kicked and rolled it in the other direction.

'Try and drop it on the rocks!' Byron shouted. 'If it breaks open the timer might be destroyed.'

He wheezed his way back to the middle where Marta was fishing around in the water for the last rope. Being slimmer than either of them, she was caught unawares by the weight of the barrel and tugged headlong over the wall. Byron flung himself on her and dragged her legs back. When she had recovered her balance she had tight hold of the rope. Behind them they heard Phil's foghorn voice;

'DOWN!'

She flung herself over him with her face buried in her arms but once more there was nothing apart from a distant crash of barrel hitting the rocks below. For a few seconds they held onto each other. He could feel her slender form trembling and gulping for breath and the recollection of Saturday evening when she had discovered Coles' body came back forcibly. But this time he could feel her genuine terror.

'Thank y-you, Byron,' she stammered, pulling herself upright with the rope. She peered out over the valley.

'It's intact,' she said. 'It's rolling down the road.'

'It'll have to look after itself; stand clear,' Phil instructed and gratefully Byron shoved himself across the road and sitting with his back to the wall he watched in a daze as the two of them struggled with the last barrel.

'Is this one bigger?' Phil demanded.

Marta shook her head. 'All five are the same.'

'Why won't it come?' The rope was strained tight over the wall.

Marta looked down into the inky blackness. 'Try pulling it across.'

They both moved to one side and letting the rope slacken off a little tugged at it. Then the other side, but still it didn't yield. They paid out the rope to almost its fullest extent and let it sink back into the depths then pulled hard to bring it back up but it stopped again at exactly the same place.

'It's caught on something,' Byron realised the moment he said it that he was stating the obvious.

'Is there enough in this to crack the wall?' Phil asked no one in particular. There was a soft whupping sound behind them. Byron dragged himself upright and looked out over the valley.

Down below, tiny, tiny car tail lights were racing up the valley towards the higher ground and safety of Blaenau Ffestiniog. More and more flashing lights were streaking around the uneven streets of Tanygrisiau and they could faintly hear the chorus of sirens. Above the helicopter heading their way.

'Go on, get moving, get them out of there,' he breathed.

'COME ON!' Phil bellowed his fear and frustration as the last barrel defied their attempts to dislodge it.

And then the quiet night erupted in an earth-shaking roar that rolled around the mountain tops.

Byron was aware of the silence. He thought his ears might have been filled with debris, but there was only a wetness seeping out of one and a feeling that a pillow had been wrapped around his head. Whatever had happened had pushed him over like a skittle. One moment he had been looking at the helicopter, the next he was lying on his back viewing the faint stars and seeing more of them in front of his eyes. He could hear a thin scream and turning saw Marta lying crumpled on the road, her face a few inches from his ear yelling at the top of her voice.

Phil was lurching forward, throwing his weight on Marta. His impressively loud bellow sounded like a tiny voice on the end of a telephone;

'STAY DOWN!'

The ground shook with another colossal roar and a flash lit up the nearby mountainsides. At any moment Byron expected to feel the road beneath him buckle and slide as the dam collapsed.

'The other one!' Marta's voice was on the end of the telephone too. She was reaching for something on the ground. Byron saw with horror she was fumbling for Phil's knife and thought for a second she was about to turn on them both.

Then in the shadow he saw she was hacking away at the last rope down by the drainage aperture. By pulling the scaffold pole she could expose a few centimetres and she feverishly sawed at it. Suddenly it fell away and the pole rolled away from the wall.

And then, in a bizarre, slow motion dream, Phil was pulling Marta upright and reaching for him. Waves of pain shot down his chest as Phil ducked under his arm and heaved him upright. Then they were staggering, running and staggering again, Phil on one side, Marta on the other dragging him towards the locked gate across the road that led back to the car. Ignoring his cries, Phil pulled him bodily onto the wall then shoved him down into the road beyond where the two of them picked him up and resumed their slow-motion run for cover.

The next blast was muted by the full depth of water and seemed to keep with Byron's slow-motion newsreel. There was a titanic bass thump like a ten mile diameter kettledrum being struck which shook the entire mountain and Stwlan lake appeared to rise up in the air as a whole. Then the centre of the lake next to the wall rose faster, reaching up and up into the night sky until it formed into an impossibly high, sharp-sided mountain which hung poised for a second before disintegrating into a ferocious rainstorm that lashed around the bowl formed by the mountain. As Byron, Phil and Marta scrambled higher up the slope toward the car, the water level dropped sharply away from the bank.

'It's burst the dam!' Byron thought fuzzily, pressing his finger into his bleeding ear. The spray had blinded him. *'We were too late!'*

But the water returned with a huge, circular wave that rushed up the bank to meet them, lapping at their feet and running back the way it had come.

'Three!' Phil screamed.

Two more to go. Could the dam survive this elemental force punching at it?

There was silence. And more silence. The silence of Maentwrog valley that always descended once everything was over.

The next twenty minutes were a haze. The helicopter hovered overhead and its searchlight played over the dam wall and finally found them huddled up at the very top of the road. Cars started arriving and flashing lights strobed over the massive bulk of the dam. Armed officers ran to them and shouted at them to lie down on their faces with their hands behind their backs. Byron just lay still and listened as at the end of a very quiet telephone, not caring what they wanted but just wishing they would go away. He could faintly hear Phil expressing himself in no uncertain terms and voices apologising; then arms reached around him and he was being gently laid on a stretcher. He felt himself swaying as he was carried to an ambulance parked at the bottom of the dam. After a much more sedate journey down he sat up and looked out of the darkened windows around at the scared people being herded out of their homes; distant sounds of children crying, soldiers running from house to house, faint sirens and flashing blue lights. And so it went on until he wound up back in Ysbyty Alltwen, back in the very room he had left a few hours earlier.

This time he didn't take any spirits with his painkillers and slept deeply.

CHAPTER 11

'HELLO SHERLOCK.'

Byron started. The distant voice was Marlene's but Marlene was back home. He struggled to sit up but had to settle for turning painfully on his side.

Marlene was in her wheelchair, picking away at a bowl of grapes on the table between them.

'I… them.' Was all he heard.

'You'll have to speak up;' he said. 'I think I've lost some hearing.'

'I know you don't like grapes so I've eaten them!' she bawled. 'You're deaf then?'

He was. One ear had been perforated by the explosion, the other was still ringing. But the consultant who had examined him whilst he slept had assured her that his hearing would return in some measure. The injured ear had a pad taped over it.

They talked but it was a difficult conversation. She wanted to say; 'I was really worried that the man I love has perished in a terrorist attack,' but everyone up and down the corridor would hear them. So she settled for;

'You look a mess.'

'How did you get here?'

She pulled her chair so her face was close to his undamaged ear. 'Chrissie brought me last night. After you rang; well I was hardly going to stay put, was I?'

'What's going on?'

She smiled proudly. 'You're big news. Top story here and across Europe. 'Dam attack foiled by off-duty detective.'

'Did the dam hold?'

She nodded. 'The whole area is evacuated until they've done a full structural survey, but it looks like the wall is intact. They're draining it down as we shout. Two of the bombs were smashed so only three went off. If all had gone off in situ the wall would have breached. There's a lot of people who want to shake your hand.'

'It's Phil and Dylan they should be thanking.'

'And me!'

'And you,' he agreed. 'Not to mention Marta… who helped eventually. Where is she?'

'Thereby hangs the question for North Wales Police. Did you see her go?'

'Marlene, love, I was lying on my back wondering if I still had a full complement of body parts. I would hardly be watching to see whether she was staying around or not.'

'Well she scarpered. In all the confusion and people fleeing in case the dam broke, she got out. I've no doubt they'll get her soon enough. And Huw, whatever his name was.'

'Not if Marta finds him first.' Marta probably still carried Coles' gun. Huw would be dead meat if she caught up with him, which was inherently satisfying. Byron lay back on the pillows and smiled.

'You liked her, didn't you?'

'Marlene, can we have this conversation some other time? Right now I just want to sleep.'

Once word got out that DI Unsworth was back in the land of the living, the phone never gave him rest. Jason was first on the line, distraught;

'We're only allowed as far as Dduallt! We can possibly run round there, but it's messed our timetables up. How long will it be restricted?'

It took a few attempts for Byron to understand him by which time Jason was hoarse. Byron placated him as patiently as possible; be realistic; the dam's structural integrity might still be compromised. Who'd want to be on a passenger train below if the remainder burst open? And think of the poor residents of Tanygrisiau who were now camped out in community halls and schools around the area.

'I'll find out how long it will be before they can reopen,' he promised. Next to him, Marlene slept. The difficult conversation was still to be had between them.

Then it was Phil. 'Just checking on you, mate.' He had little need to exert his voice.

'No lasting damage,' Byron reported. 'But I might be a bit deaf on the right side.'

'Hell of a bang, wasn't it?'

'That's one way to describe it.' Even now Byron could recall that colossal eruption of noise and light. 'Did the folk down below think the dam had gone?'

'Yes. It was chaos. One moment the police were having difficulty convincing them there was danger, the next they were quite literally running for high ground. The evacuation plan was good, though. They funnelled them up the sides of the hill where they'd have been safer. But the commander I spoke to thought his time had come when he saw the explosions.'

'Same here. I'm surprised it held.'

'It held 'cause you used your brain, mate. Whilst I was too busy getting those barrels out, you had the bright idea of throwing them off the edge. If they'd been together when they went up…'

Byron shivered. 'I'm glad two of them broke. How's Dylan?'

'I'm on my way to find out. I'll be in touch.'

There were more calls, press, national and local media. He woke Marlene who cannily fielded them to Gwillim's secretary – after all it was his show and with Byron's deafness it was impossible to hold a conversation anyway. Let him arrange a press conference. Byron would give a statement but he would agree the wording with all involved. After all this was a political attack. Questions were being asked in the House; the cabinet was in special briefing and speculation about who the plotters were was rife. Gwillim's PA promised to get him to ring them as soon as she could contact him.

Christine called by and seeing the amount of attention Byron was receiving applied herself to her sister, fussing around until Marlene despatched her on an unnecessary errand just to get her away for a while.

'Where's she staying?'

'Your landlady contacted me before you woke up. Wanted to know you were in one piece and what could she do to help. So Chrissie got your room. It was going free,' she added, defensively.

Byron shrugged, then wished he hadn't as pain shot down his back. 'Makes sense, I suppose.'

Gwillim rang back, sounding harassed but slightly incredulous that something as inconsequential as a lone suicide could conceal such potentially catastrophic outcomes.

'I take it I should disregard your first report,' was his final bellowed remark before ringing off. Byron couldn't decide if he was serious or not.

The earliest television pictures made for spectacular viewing. An intrepid reporter had been alerted to the situation in time to be present with a video camera. From the distance, the mountains were dark, even in the moonlight and the dam a black bar across the valley. Suddenly the darkness was torn by two flashes followed half a second later by thunderclaps that boomed and rolled down the mountainside.

'Is the dam going to hold?' the reporter asked a nearby soldier. The reply was heavily bleeped.

'You're lucky it did,' murmured Byron, 'standing where you were.'

The current news coverage showed live pictures from Stwlan Dam from that morning. The lake level was considerably lower than last night and people were asking if it was indeed leaking. A spokesman from the Power Station assured them that the top lake was being drained as a precaution prior to checking the dam interior wall. A large chunk had been ripped out of two of the central supports at the base of the exterior wall, but no structural cracks were present. Byron's face flashed up from a mugshot supplied by Avon and Somerset Force which must have been years out of date and an even more regrettable one of Phil Braithewaite in combat fatigues. No wonder they had been mistaken for terrorists, Byron thought. Pictures of Dylan and Marta followed, unfortunately next to each other so that it looked like they were co-conspirators followed by diagrams showing where the explosives had been placed and what the effect would have been had they detonated as planned. Someone in graphics must have got up early, Byron smiled to himself, as the computer-generated dam cracked and water poured through the gap, tearing the structure apart.

After the newsreel had rolled round for the third time, Byron turned it off and went to sleep. About an hour later a sound disturbed him. Marlene had turned it back on.

More television coverage had emerged – the recorded video from the helicopter was impressive. It had been flying up towards Stwlan when the first bomb exploded. The cockpit was filled with shouts as the chopper was thrown up and away from the dam face. Fortunately the pilot was able to recover control and the second and third explosions were recorded from a safer distance. The sight of the plume of water rising hundreds of feet into the air was unforgettable.

'I was there…' Byron murmured in disbelief.

His phone rang. Byron wearily handed it to Marlene. 'Tell whoever it is I'm not available,' he said.

She chatted at some length to whoever it was and Byron grew curious. '*Who is it?*' he mouthed.

It was Dylan. Propped up in the orthopaedic ward at Ysbyty Gwynedd in Bangor. His neck was immobilised and he had broken three ribs but was his customary irrepressible self. Marlene relayed his messages.

'He says do you want to do the Gravity Train again?'

Byron shouted, 'I'll give it a few weeks. How long you out of action for?'

Couple of months, at least, was his answer. Then Marlene relayed;

'Phil Braithewaite came by. Left him a certificate of some sort that the volunteers made this morning. What's it for, Dylan?'

His answer made her smile. 'I'm not to tell you. You've got one too.'

'I can't wait!'

From then on the interruptions followed thick and fast. A battery of media and press camped out in the hospital car park and demanding access for an interview. Senior detectives, accompanied by military bigwigs mouthing profuse apologies about disturbing him in hospital and so on. Marlene managed to supply most of the detail as they pieced events together, but Byron, still hearing everything like on the end of a telephone had to supply the missing bits.

'Mrs Unsworth,' Sandy Constance of the Welsh Anti Terrorist Unit said as they prepared to leave. 'We're really sorry to have to do this when your husband is still injured, but we need as much information on Marta Kowalczyk and Huw Davies, whatever his real name may be, as possible to get to the channel ports and airports. If you could let us know anything else he may recall it would be appreciated. In the meantime, a press conference has been arranged for Mr Braithewaite to brief the media. I take it your husband won't mind attending that?'

No, Marlene assured him, Byron would cope with her help.

Then Phil who showed up prior to the press conference clutching a huge bouquet of flowers for Marlene and a selection of Danish pastries for them both. The television was back on when he arrived and the rolling headlines were proclaiming the biggest manhunt of the decade for the 'Dam busters.' Scenes from the evacuation of the village were harrowing. The explosions set off a panic that conveyed itself through the reporter to the viewer. They were followed by a video taken from Facebook showing Byron and

Dylan, their hi-viz jackets gleaming brightly in the dusk, exiting the Gravity Train at Rhiw Goch.

'It just beggars belief you both survived that fall,' Phil said, as the slow-mo replay showed Byron gracefully forward flip into the darkness followed by a shattering crash as the wagons disintegrated.

'I find it amazing that every little mishap is recorded for posterity,' Marlene grumbled. 'There they are, about to witness what could be a double fatality and what do they do? Record it so they can upload it to the net.'

The television commentary was trying to link the Gravity Train incident with the subsequent Dam attack. Phil listened and snorted.

'Sooner we get this press conference going the better. If I heard that right they've just implied that you two were trying to raise the alarm about the dam by hitching a ride on some wagons.'

'At least you can hear,' Byron groaned. A sharp pain had invaded his ear and the doctor on his rounds had sent for some antibiotics.

'Count yourself lucky,' Phil replied. 'That was one of the biggest blasts I have witnessed since they blew up an arms dump in Helmand Province. You were looking out across the valley and shielded by the wall. If you had been looking over the edge it would have torn your head clean off.'

The press conference was endured by Byron who just wanted a bath and to go back to sleep. Marlene, however, enjoyed it immensely. With Phil's help she pieced the story together from the beginning as the cameras rolled and the mob of photographers snapped away; starting with the discovery of Coles' body and the sheep on the line and related how that her husband's enquiring mind had picked up the minor discrepancies that had led to the discovery of the plot.

'He's like a terrier,' she declared, as Phil was trying not to laugh. 'He worries at any and every detail until he gets to the truth. It was fortunate he was on hand to investigate this one!' Next to her,

Phil nudged her and Byron gazed blankly into space not hearing a word anyway.

'You smug, lying toad,' Phil breathed as he turned away from the rostrum and wheeled her back to their room.

She turned her dark eyes on him with a hurt expression. 'I'm just making sure credit goes where it's due.'

Byron, however, got the message when, two days later with his less damaged ear much improved he was able to listen to his wife's performance at the press conference.

The recording of the conference finished and he switched it off and turned to face her. 'Okay, so you've proved you're indispensable, now what?'

She flushed. 'I'm glad you've reached that conclusion on your own.'

'You want to know what happened between me and Marta, is that it?'

She brushed the folds of her skirt out on her lap. 'I already know what happened on Moel y Gest.'

'What?'

'Nothing. I know you too well, Byron. You were always a ladies' man but first and foremost you are a husband and a father. It would take a lot to break that up. But I would like to know what sort of nothing took place.'

He told her; her well-acted distress, carefully contrived outrage to get him to divulge their investigations. She interrupted him.

'You know I don't mean that.'

So he told her how Marta had clung to him, held on to him and kissed him. She listened intently.

'Marta played on your weakness – our weakness.'

'What weakness?'

'I'm hardly a wife to you any more am I?' She had flushed deeper. 'An invalid, like this? Marta knew that was a chink in your armour and exploited it. She knew that if you felt attracted to her as a vulnerable, lonely woman who flirted with you, you would let your guard down. But she didn't reckon on the backlash.'

'Which was..?'

'On the dam. She had the gun. She could have walked away and left you two to die up there. Why did she stay?'

'She was angry about Huw, scared, out of her depth…'

Marlene smiled sadly. 'You can be the thickest detective alive sometimes. Marta might have started out to manipulate you but soon she wasn't play-acting anymore. She was in love with you.'

'In love… you're having me on!'

'Byron, I broke off what was very nearly an engagement for you. Okay, it was years ago but some things don't change. You're tubby, going very grey and hardly the catch of the day…'

'Tell it the way it is, why don't you?'

She went on; 'but there's always been something about you that makes me feel I'm the luckiest woman alive. I think she felt that too and reacted accordingly.'

'I'm not sure what you really mean.'

Marlene sighed; the sigh of a woman who rather wishes she didn't have to explain herself. Finally she said;

'It's not your appearance, your intellect or anything like that. It's just the way you are. Chrissie says the same – you're just… well… dependable. You know what I mean? There as a Dad when the kids were young, now with the grandchildren you're there. Not doing amazing things but just giving a feel of…' she struggled for an appropriate word but it eluded her and she had to settle for a lame; 'being fatherly. It's written all over you and a lot of my friends say the same. Women notice that, and Marta felt it too. She needed someone like you. That's why she couldn't walk away.'

'Hmm!' Byron tried to sound unconvinced but inwardly felt rather pleased, until she said;

'But you step out of line again and I'll scratch your eyes out.'

CHAPTER 12

TWO WEEKS LATER the attack on Stwlan dam was old news, at least for the wider world. Local people still made their way to the Harbour station with tokens of appreciation for the 'Brave detective who saved their town.' Byron's office was layered with cards; hand-drawn from local children, small notes, a large card signed by the volunteers and staff of the railway and numerous gifts ranging from the edible and useful to things he would give away at the first opportunity. Marlene was outside Spooners indulging in a very out of hours large white wine and enjoying the sunshine. In a few minutes the midday train would arrive and they would board first class with Dylan. A presentation would be held at Tanygrisiau with the top brass of the railway, power station and local dignitaries to celebrate the reopening of the line and acknowledge their vital contribution.

His phone pinged. Message from Marlene. *'Dylan's here.'*

Dylan resisted any assistance to board the carriage. Awkwardly he heaved himself up the step and lunged into the nearest comfy armchair. Byron manoeuvred Marlene into another chair alongside and sat down.

'I'll go and get us some refreshments when we're underway,' he murmured. Marlene laid a hand on his arm.

'No you won't. We're guests today. It's all laid on.' She was glad she didn't have to raise her voice much now. As long as his left ear was nearest he could hear normally.

'Here comes Sergeant Pepper,' Dylan grinned as the short wiry form of Phil passed in front of the huge curved windows of the Observation Carriage. 'So he's not driving today then.'

'Not dressed like that,' Marlene observed.

Byron turned to Dylan. 'Other half is coming, is she?'

'Oh yeah. She's been looking forward to this for days. Best dress, taking pictures all over the place – yer she comes now.'

Outside Phil gallantly assisted a petite red-head up the carriage step before following himself. Introductions followed and Marlene directed Jenny, as she was called, to a comfortable seat next to her where they spent much of the journey deep in conversation.

'Merc's going to be a few days yet,' Phil announced glumly. 'They think they might have found some parts in America.'

'What's the matter with it?' Byron wanted to know. He was told that a stone had punched through a headlight and wiped out the water pump behind. 'Still,' he continued, brightening, 'the Power Station are more than happy to foot the bill and have offered a complete respray. The old girl won't know herself.'

It was a special train in every sense of the word. Just a few carriages, not scheduled in the public timetable and comprising the first class observation car, a couple of new coaches and a buffet car. David Lloyd George was at the head and after a lot of activity in the coaches behind they set off with a jerk across the Cob.

'Go easy with the old fellow...' Byron heard Phil wince.

And then the first of the silver service dining began. Outside the bright sunny weather obliged them, inside the tuxedoed waiters and waitresses plied them with expensive nibbles, appetisers and a champagne that Marlene expertly pronounced to be a very exclusive vintage. On top of the wine she had not long consumed, Marlene was becoming garrulous and not a little tipsy. Every now and then she and Jenny would explode with laughter and look round at them. Byron suspected they were comparing menfolk.

'Did they charge Janice?' Byron asked Dylan. He munched another canapé before answering;

'I think the old hag might get away with it. She maintains ignorance of the illegal contents of the hidden account – well she claims that John used it as a means of ensuring her cooperation. I believe her... not!'

'I have to admit I feel rather sorry for her,' said Byron mildly. 'She can't claim the money.'

Phil laughed. 'And you pity the toxic Marta, too, I daresay. She seems to have comprehensively vanished off the face of the earth.'

Byron shuffled uncomfortably. He had tried messaging Marta on his mobile; messages such as, *'There's still justice in England. We can put your side across.'* Not that he expected any reply. Marta would not use her phone for fear of being tracked. He kept these communications strictly between himself and the anti-terrorist squad leading the manhunt. He wasn't sure they approved of this unorthodox means of communication, but they did promise more than a fair hearing for her if she gave herself up. Nothing had come back until she sent yesterday's terse question;

'Phil said I wasn't a killer?'

His reply had been equally concise;

'Huw is more use to us alive.'

That was yesterday. Nothing since.

'She was no dumb blonde,' he remarked. 'Honours degree in Modern Languages at Warsaw Uni. Then a post graduate in European Culture.' Marta's life had been picked over by the tabloids and he had followed it closely. How could a bright, high-achieving young woman fall so far? Next to him Phil chuckled.

'And I called her stupid!'

'Well she was being foolish.' He nearly added, *'love does that to people.'*

Phil was imbibing more champagne and becoming mischievous.

'So there am I, telling her how stupid she is, and she's about to leave us to it. In fact…' he took another swig of champagne and laughed too loudly, 'I was lucky she didn't put a bullet in me for my insolence. But what does Casanova here do?'

Byron squirmed. Behind him Marlene and Jenny were putting the world to rights so he hoped they wouldn't overhear.

'He just schmoozes up to her and she turns to putty in his arms. I tell you, Byron's got it, whatever it may be.'

Another gale of laughter from behind. Hopefully Marlene had missed that comment. Byron tried to move the conversation on. He nudged Dylan gently, avoiding his ribs.

'Penrhyn station. Bring back fond memories?' The train wasn't due to stop here so they watched the little station crawl past, followed immediately by the road crossing and shortly afterwards Rhiw Goch.

'There's the new bit of wall,' Phil pointed and Marlene and Jenny broke off their gossip to look over the edge at the pristine stonework that marked the exit route of the runaway wagon. Byron looked through the window over the edge of the viaduct and shuddered. The wood had been cleared and the forest floor was a long way down. High enough to set his vertigo off.

'Can you believe we jumped off there?' he murmured.

'I hope you've got a good life policy on Dylan,' Marlene said to Jenny. 'I understand he wants to try it again.'

'Mad, that one,' she sighed and they went back to their previous conversation.

'How long before the dam refills?' Dylan asked. 'I think everyone is fed up with the power shortages by now.'

'Next week;' Phil seemed well-informed on progress up at Stwlan. Contractors with huge floodlights had been working day and night to repair and check the structure. A lot of water had been lost over the spillway of the lower lake and so full capacity would not be possible until some decent rainfall filled both lakes up again. For once, the Blaenau area was praying for a bout of Welsh weather.

The first of a few courses arrived on silver trays. Tables had been set out with sparkling white cloths and rather unnecessary candles. They sat down and enjoyed the sheer luxury.

'Well this is a bit of all right,' Dylan remarked, spreading his pork and wild mushroom pâté lavishly over his toast.

'You think this is good?' Byron replied. 'You should try the Fish and Chip special on Wednesday evenings.'

'What awaits us at Tanygrisiau?' asked Jenny as the conversation flagged.

Marlene giggled. 'Have you seen 'The Railway Children?''

'A long time ago,' she replied.

'There's that bit when the kids save the train from the landslide and get met off the train by an oompah band and the Board of Directors to be presented with a watch.' Marlene chortled. 'I'm hoping it's going to be like that. You know, we line up for a commemorative watch and a solemn handshake and all the time the band keep starting and stopping.'

'And Byron has to make a speech!' Phil chuckled. 'But he's not to accept any money as that wouldn't be right and proper.'

'You good for a speech, mate?' Phil wanted to know. But Byron wasn't listening. The train was climbing towards Moelwyn Tunnel. He'd passed this point many times since the incident and each time a sense of sadness washed over him. John Coles died alone in the last carriage of the down train. They now knew he had been killed by an ex-colleague he had known from the years he worked in South Africa. A freelancer like himself who got a taste for easy money and had invited Coles on board his scheme. The threads of the plot were long and complex but it was suspected that agents working on behalf of a consortium of European energy suppliers were involved, making capital of Britain's shortfall. If UK power was seriously compromised, the country would be ready to pay anything to keep the lights on and they would be on hand to supply it at grossly inflated prices. The attack on the Peak Storage facility was intended to force the issue and remove any bargaining power the country might have. So explosives were needed, and a lot of them. The proposed dam schemes provided a perfect cover and Huw Davies, or whatever his real name was, was recruited to supply the logistics for the attack.

Whilst the new hydro-electric scheme proposals and associated rumpus were coincidental, it was excellent timing. One failed dam would make building newer ones much more difficult. The UK energy supply would be in limp mode for years and dependent on imported electricity – so much so that it might become addicted to it rather than develop a home-grown solution. The consequences of the attack, had it succeeded, would have lasted for decades. But now, grumpily, the various Government departments responsible were talking to each other and a strategy for a secure power supply was becoming possible – one that might include educating the country towards turning the lights off themselves.

Why had Coles fallen foul of the rest of the conspirators? The most likely answer was that he had been kept ignorant of why they needed the explosive, but had begun to guess the truth. His forays up to the dam, recorded on the CCTV records back at the power station showed him a week before pacing the dam, inspecting the structure and making notes. Whatever his deductions it had boiled down to that single, enigmatic phrase;

'1000 to bring it down at 10.'

Coles was corrupt, of that there was no doubt, but why had he bailed? Perhaps he could not bear to imagine the consequences of his actions. But he needed to get out without his part being exposed. An anonymous note, with clear details of the proposed attack was his most likely next step, but the conspirators beat him to it, just a few yards from where they now were, steaming through the long tunnel just prior to the summit. Wrenching the door open and pressing an identical gun to his against his head had been the work of a few seconds. All it then took was to wrap his fingers around the butt and retrieve Coles' own weapon from his rucksack and the 'suicide' was complete.

Maybe John Coles loved this part of the world too much as well, Byron decided.

As they emerged into the bright sunlight on the shores of the lower lake, Byron looked around at the changes to the area. Plant and machinery surrounded the power station and trucks rumbled up the steep roads. A lot of essential maintenance had been rescheduled whilst the station was out of action. Further up the mountain, out of sight from the track, cranes and scaffolding swathed the dam. Byron wanted to take a walk up to see, but he was still a little weak. The village itself had returned to normal; traffic, the Lakeside café with a host of motorbikes outside and the occasional bus grumbling round the tiny streets.

'Ladies and gentlemen,' the train manager, himself resplendent in tuxedo and tails for the event, broke in on Byron's reflections. 'we do hope you are enjoying your time with us…'

The raucous chorus of agreement drowned his words, he waited to continue.

'In a few moments we will alight at Tanygrisiau where there will be a short ceremony to express the gratitude of the staff and directors of quite a few companies around here. There will be a presentation after which we will serve the main courses of your meal. Dessert, should you have room – and we hope you will, will be served on the return journey.'

'Do you want to see our tickets?' Dylan asked, his voice a little too loud. ''Cause my lady, yer, she thinks she might have lost 'ers.'

'Oh Dylan, behave!' Jenny poked him in the ribs. He yelped. 'What do you think you'll get? Not a watch, I hope, you keep losing them, look.'

Phil and Byron exchanged glances. A couple of days back Phil had approached Byron on this very subject and Byron had had no difficulty recommending a suitable reward.

'Get him Society life membership,' he suggested. 'I think he'll like that.'

Phil tinged a wine glass with a spoon. 'Before we arrive, ladies and gentlemen can I, on behalf of the volunteers of the Ffestiniog Railway, make a small presentation to a man who up until recently has had the reputation of being the most sensible and sedate of our staff. I'm talking of course of Byron Unsworth, the hero of the hour and reason why we still have a railway left to run.'

'Get on with it,' growled Byron.

'Those of you who know Byron will know that he takes his duties as an upholder of law and order very seriously. He is conscientious, never prone to reckless or impulsive behaviour and a model of probity and decency. In fact he is an example to us all.'

He washed a mouthful of champagne around his mouth then continued; 'so when we calculated the speed that Byron and his sidekick PC Woods here managed to achieve on the Gravity Train, many of our regulars could not believe that it was the self-same man who had achieved it. Apart from, of course, not completing the course, which we will overlook on this occasion, they achieved a track record of,' with a flourish he produced a framed certificate and read from it;

'Fastest Gravity Train descent in Ffestiniog history. Seven and a half miles in eighteen minutes. Average speed twenty-five miles an hour.'

He placed the framed certificate in Byron's hands amidst applause. Byron was about to respond in kind when his phone buzzed. A message from Marta. He glanced at it them jumped to his feet.

'I need to answer this' he said. 'Excuse me,' he said and hurried out to the corridor.

'There's always a first time.'

His heart sank. She'd tracked Huw down. Well, he had it coming. The phone buzzed again.

'But not this time.' This had photos attached.

The first was the green carriage. It was stashed away outside Boston Lodge workshops, looking somewhat dejected. It would be put back into service once the police released it and its melancholy associations had faded. The second showed a body, trussed up and laid on the back seat where Coles had died. The third was of an old-style mobile phone.

'Gwen, it's me, Byron. Is DC Young there? Good, tell him this is urgent. He's about to make the arrest of his career. Get him to

Boston Lodge workshops. The old green carriage... yes, drop whatever he's doing and go.'

He returned to the carriage. For a moment he considered telling them there and then, but the train was slowing and outside he could hear the Jazz band that entertained the Summer evening specials striking up.

It would wait until they were back on their way. He would enjoy telling them.

The more he thought about it, the more he relished the way Marta had done this. Huw was probably marched at gunpoint in the early hours of the morning and tied up in the same spot where Coles had met his end. What reason would he have to believe she wasn't going to do for him there and then?

The train stopped with a squeal of brakes and the doors were flung open.

'You coming, love?' Called Marlene through the open door.

'Come on mate, you'll have to face them, they won't go away,' Phil boomed.

He looked at the pictures again. Huw must have been terrified! He knew it was wrong, but the thought sent a delicious shiver down his spine.

CHAPTER 13

'YOU KNOW THIS IS JUST BONKERS?'

'I know,' she said, 'and bizarre, and sad, and why don't I just accept things as they are and stop making a fool of myself; yada, yada…' She yelped as the rugged wheelchair hit a rock and bounced sideways.

Behind them the helicopter rotors had ceased turning. A few hikers had assembled to view the unusual scenario. Normally rescue choppers picked injured people up from mountain ridges and spirited them away. This one had disgorged a woman in a heavy duty wheelchair along with a handful of brawny men and one who looked down the steeply sloping sides with growing unease.

'You okay, madam?' Geoff, one of the marines from Phil Braithewaite's old unit steadied the chair and its occupant.

'I'm fine,' Marlene said. 'No, really, I am. I took double dose of painkillers about an hour back so I wouldn't notice if you pushed me off the side.'

'We'll try to avoid that happening, ma'am,' said the marine on the other side of the wheelchair. 'You okay, Sir?' He had caught sight of the grey pallor on Byron's face.

Marlene laughed. 'Oh don't mind my husband. He just gets a bit wobbly up here. Now I don't want anyone putting themselves at risk for my sake. We go up as far as is practicable, okay?'

'Understood, ma'am.' Geoff cast another look at Byron who was walking up the exact middle of the slope that led from the wide shoulder to the sharp pinnacle of Cnicht Mountain. He took deliberate strides and kept his eyes somewhere in mid-distance. Every step narrowed the path and it became increasingly difficult not to see the sharply sloping sides that gave the mountain its striking front aspect. To their left the gradient fell away into steep rock-faces and the next sight of ground was the inclined plane of the track far away on the other side of the valley that once served as another route for the slate to be brought down the mountainside. The trouble was it was so far down, and he felt so exposed and tiny up here on this rocky peak.

'I'm fine,' he muttered to himself, biting his lip each time he said it. *'Just fine. What is the chance of my falling off? Next to nil. It's dry, sunny, very little breeze, conditions perfect. There's nothing to worry about.'*

And yet Byron felt the familiar sense of dread; the tightening in his belly, the pain running down the back of his legs and the weird feeling that the solid rock was slipping around beneath his feet. He walked ahead, wondering why he had allowed Marlene to talk him into this caper.

A week ago, they had been presented with tokens of appreciation from the power industry that ran the Peak Storage facility. There had been discussions at the time, between management executives and Marlene, that Byron had not been party to. Something had been arranged and it was not until a few days later he found out what she had asked for.

'A helicopter will set us down on the shoulder, some six hundred metres from the summit;' her eyes had sparkled at the news. 'And Phil's got some mates who'll bounce me as far up as they can. It'll be like old times, won't it? I never thought this would be possible again.' Byron tried to look enthusiastic as she went on; 'Okay, it's not quite like when we used to walk up from Tanny, but it's better than nothing.'

'Do you really need me to come as well?' Byron asked hopefully.

She smiled sweetly. 'Pretend I'm Marta if it helps. You didn't get vertigo with her, I presume?'

'How low can you stoop?' he had protested. 'That was Moel y Gest which is not steep, or exposed or the sort of place you fall off.'

'Darling, you'll have four marines, a helicopter and me to help you. Look, maybe you can go down by chopper, I'll make my own way down.'

'Yeah, sure.'

'Say you'll do it.' She fluttered her eyelashes shamelessly at him and he reluctantly agreed.

As Byron strode ahead, keeping his eyes fixed on the small flat area of scuffed grass that marked the very top of Cnicht, he could hear the marines grunting and cursing behind him. He had explained and they had readily accepted that he could be of no earthly use to them. Their instructions were to proceed as far as possible and call him back if they couldn't go the whole way. The summit was now only a hundred metres away but between him and their goal the path spitefully narrowed, leaving an exposed track just a few metres wide across which he had to walk. Slowly, turning his feet on the spot he shuffled round hoping that Marlene's retinue had got as far as they were going to go.

'Move on Bonington!' Marlene was just behind him. The wheelchair had been abandoned and Alfie, the burliest marine, had her small form cradled in his arms. She was never a great weight, but he made carrying her look easy.

Byron turned back to look at the path ahead. He could feel more colour draining from his face and a horrible feeling he was going to pass out.

'Hold my hand,' Marlene called. 'You'll be just fine.' She tugged his elbow and he jumped nervously. Slowly, placing his hand in hers he stepped out into the void.

It took some time to cross the narrow section, during which a family with two teenage children came the other way, skipped past them and disappeared in the direction of the helicopter, possibly hoping for a ride. Marlene's handlers gave him more attention, alternately coaxing and teasing him. But finally they were on the small plateau that was the summit of Cnicht. Alfie set her down facing out over Porthmadog. She patted the ground next to her and with relief Byron settled himself down, his fingers surreptitiously gripping the rocky projections either side of him.

'Ten minutes,' Marlene instructed and they retreated to crack open cans of beer back by the chopper.

She nestled herself against him. 'Thank you,' she murmured in his good ear.

'For what?'

'Indulging me, like this. I know you're scared...'

'Terrified more like. But I know this means a lot to you.'

'I... I really never thought I'd ever get up here again. I'm sorry, I'm being silly,' she sniffed. 'Have you got a tissue?'

'Have my sleeve,' he offered. She buried her face in his shirt and sobbed. 'What is it about me that makes women cry?' he wondered aloud.

'I'm sorry, love,' she repeated. 'It's all sort of catching up on me. You know... what nearly happened to you. I keep seeing you and Dylan flying through the air; I had a dream last night; I was watching you jump off the gravity train and nobody seemed bothered so I had to crawl down and find you and you were... you weren't moving. You were all twisted and still.'

'Well I'm only deaf, not dead. Huw's in custody, Marta's vanished into thin air and we're alive. With a bit of luck Avon and Somerset will let me go out on a high note then we can spend some more time together. How does that make you feel?'

She didn't reply for a few minutes and he took the time to look out over the panorama before them; the craggy mountain profile above Harlech off to their left giving place to the broad sweep of the estuary ahead and the grander mountains of Moel Hebog to their right with Snowdon in the clouds beyond. The air was still and clear. Far below some forestry work was in progress and a lazy plume of smoke drifted across the pine plantations above Croesor.

'I'd like that;' she withdrew her face from his shirt and examined the damp patch she'd left there. 'Jill was asking about when you thought you'd retire so she can recruit us for babysitting.' Jill was their oldest child married to Owain and living in

Carmarthen and their two lively kids were too much for Marlene to cope with on her own.

'I'll play the post traumatic stress card if needs be,' Byron suggested. 'Give them the option of me carrying on but spending all my time at Occupational Health or off their hands altogether if the price is right.'

'I just love this place,' she murmured and lapsed into silence, punctuated by the occasional sniff. Byron felt his vertigo easing slightly and looked around. The valley to the left was impossibly green – the warm summer had been preceded by a wet spring and the slopes were still soaking up the run off from the numerous peat bogs high above. Directly ahead the path to Croesor dropped sharply down what was termed a 'scramble' meaning you slid down on your backside scrabbling for toeholds until the ground levelled out. He had done it twice before when his vertigo wasn't so crippling but couldn't face that way down now. Far in the distance the blue-grey sea and the tiny line of the Cob. A steam train was crossing it; a minuscule puff of white inching its way towards the harbour station to unload another twelve or so carriages of holidaymakers after their journey.

Byron watched its progress absently. The boy with tousled red hair, his face wet and sooty, sprang to mind, eagerly hanging out of the window to catch a glimpse of the engine. How many boys and girls like that were on this train, feeling that same thrill of a ride on a train pulled by an locomotive that chuffed and snorted and belched smoke – unlike the sanitised modern electric and diesel locos. There was something timeless and yet living about a steam engine and it gratified him immensely to see new generations of converts to the heritage railways.

Try as he might, though, he couldn't stop recalling John Coles slumped in that last carriage. A dirty, shameful business that could have ended so differently if Marlene hadn't badgered him to dig deeper into his apparent suicide. How much of the Ffestiniog railway would still be traversible if Stwlan dam had ruptured? He glanced at her. She was absorbed in the panorama before her, lapping up the view she had given up ever seeing again.

'Wouldn't be much railway left without you,' she said, prising his fingers off their grip on the rock and slipping her hand into his. 'That dam burst would have probably closed over half of the track.'

'How d'you do that?' He asked, startled. 'Read my mind like that?'

She chuckled. 'An educated guess. You were watching the train on the Cob. With what's just happened, I could see what you'd be thinking.'

'You're amazing.'

'I know. So what did Huw confess to in the end?'

'Pretty much as expected. He was a go-between for a cartel of energy wheeler-dealers looking to cripple the UK generating capacity. They tried cyber attacks a while back but the networks are too resilient now so they went back to basics. They recruited Coles to supply them explosives, under the counter as it were, telling him they were for illegal mining. But Coles got too suspicious for his own good. They spotted him many times up by Stwlan Dam near where they had hidden the cache of explosives in a mineshaft and realised he had worked out what their intention was. So they had to get rid of him in a way that provoked as little suspicion as possible.'

She snuggled against him. 'Starting with a bunch of sheep. Reckon they'll be caught?'

Byron reflected. 'Huw and Marta were only small fry but look how well they covered their tracks. I imagine their paymasters would be much more difficult to find. Anyway...' He let go her hand, stretched himself then remembered he was on top of a high mountain and hastily renewed his grip on the rock; 'it's not my problem any more.'

They both knew their time was limited. Soon the helicopter engine would roar into life and the downdraught would flatten the grass and scrub for many metres around. It would whisk them away from this tranquil spot and back to normality; to the remaining days of his volunteer stint during which Marlene and her sister would enjoy an unexpected bonus of a luxury hotel break paid for by the generating company and he would finish off his duties with the railway.

It was peaceful here. He felt little need to talk, neither did Marlene. They cuddled together enjoying the moment until, wafted heavenwards on an updraught they both heard it together; a long, keening wail, ricocheting off the naked rocky slopes, drawn out by the journey from the railway to this lonely peak.

'They're calling us,' he said, rising uneasily to his feet and signalling to the men clustered near the chopper. 'Time to go.'

Printed in Great Britain
by Amazon

73241879R00106